Cal Stood By The Sitting Room Windows, Taking In The Frozen Cityscape.

Devon's breath caught as she went to stand beside him. Buildings, trees, the statues on the bridge, the river itself…everything as far as the eye could see lay under a blanket of glistening white. Not a single car or bus or snowplow moved through the frozen stillness.

"Looks like most of the city must be shut down," Devon murmured, awestruck.

"Guess we'll have to resort to plan B," said Cal.

"Which is?"

"We talk politics. We try to guess each other's favorite movies. We wrap up in blankets and share our body heat. We have wild, uninhibited sex."

Her jaw dropped.

"We don't have to follow that precise order," he informed her solemnly. "We could start with the sex and work our way backward."

Dear Reader,

If you've never visited Germany or Austria during the Christmas season, you've missed something really special. Think Kris Kringle, angelic choirs singing "Silent Night" and outdoor markets crammed with beautiful handicrafts and the most scrumptious eats imaginable. What better place to strand a heroine who's completely turned off by the way Christmas has been commercialized, and a hero who decides on the spot she's all he wants under his tree!

Here's hoping you, too, enjoy the beauty of this season and the powerful message of love and joy that comes with it.

And be sure to watch for more HOLIDAYS ABROAD. *The Duke's New Year Resolution* is coming next month from the Silhouette Desire line, followed by *The Executive's Valentine Seduction.*

Best,

Merline Lovelace

MERLINE LOVELACE

THE CEO'S CHRISTMAS PROPOSITION

Silhouette® Desire

Published by Silhouette Books
America's Publisher of Contemporary Romance

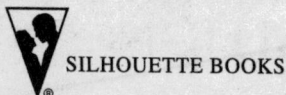

SILHOUETTE BOOKS

ISBN-13: 978-0-373-76905-6
ISBN-10: 0-373-76905-9

THE CEO'S CHRISTMAS PROPOSITION

Recent Books by Merline Lovelace

Silhouette Desire

*Full Throttle #1556
†Devlin and the Deep Blue Sea #1726
**The CEO's Christmas Proposition #1905

Silhouette Romantic Suspense

*A Question of Intent #1255
*The Right Stuff #1279
†Diamonds Can Be Deadly #1411
†Closer Encounters #1439
*Stranded with a Spy #1483
†Match Play #1500
†Undercover Wife #1531

Silhouette Nocturne

Mind Games #33

†Code Name: Danger
*To Protect and Defend
**Holidays Abroad

MERLINE LOVELACE

A retired air force officer, Merline Lovelace served at bases all over the world, including tours in Taiwan, Vietnam and at the Pentagon. When she hung up her uniform for the last time, she decided to combine her love of adventure with a flair for storytelling, basing many of her tales on her experiences in the service.

Since then, she's produced more than seventy action-packed novels, many of which have made the *USA TODAY* and Waldenbooks bestseller lists. Over ten million copies of her works are in print in 31 countries. Named Oklahoma's Writer of the Year and the Oklahoma Female Veteran of the Year, Merline is also a recipient of Romance Writers of America's prestigious RITA® Award.

When she's not glued to her keyboard, she and husband enjoy traveling and chasing little white balls around the fairways of Oklahoma. Check her Web site at www.merlinelovelace.com for news, contests and information about upcoming releases.

To Pat, my college roomie who went off to Germany without me all those years ago but made up for it with four decades of friendship. Al and I still owe you and Norbert for the barn concert and dinner on the Elbe!

One

Shoulders hunched against the icy sleet pounding Germany's Dresden International Airport, Devon McShay grimaced at the Christmas carols belting from the outdoor loudspeakers.

"Okay," she muttered under her breath. "Call me Mrs. Scrooge. Call me the Grinchette. Call me the ultimate Krank. I hate this time of year."

Well, that wasn't totally true. The hopeless idealist in her still wanted to believe people might someday actually heed the messages of joy and peace the season signified. *If* they could get past the crass commercialization, that is. Not to mention the hole they dug for themselves every year by splurging on gifts they couldn't afford.

Her parents' increasingly bitter arguments over finances had always peaked this time of year and led eventually to an even more bitter divorce. Christmases after that had become a battleground, with each parent trying to outdo the other to win a daughter's love.

Devon's own holiday track record was just as dismal. As she sloshed through ankle-deep slush toward the terminal, she shook her head at her incredible idiocy in falling for a too-handsome, too-cocky newscaster at Dallas's Channel Six. Silly her, she'd actually thought she'd broken the Christmas curse when Blake caught her under the mistletoe and slipped a diamond on her finger. Exactly one year later, she'd walked into the station to find her husband with his hand under the miniskirt of a female Santa and his tongue halfway down her throat.

Devon had put her jerk of an ex out of her life, but even now, three years later, she couldn't work up any enthusiasm for colored lights or eggnog. That's why she'd jumped at the chance to avoid yet another season of forced Christmas cheer when her friend and business partner came down with the flu yesterday, mere hours before she was supposed to leave for Germany.

Devon, Sabrina Russo and Caroline Walters had been friends before they became business partners. They'd met while spending their junior year at the University of Salzburg. Filled with the dreams and enthusiasm of youth, the three coeds had formed a fast friendship.

They'd maintained that friendship long-distance in the years that followed. Until last May, when they'd met for a minireunion. After acknowledging that their lives so far hadn't lived up to their dreams, they'd decided to pool resources, educational backgrounds and interests. Two months later, they'd quit their respective jobs, relocated to Virginia and launched European Business Services, Incorporated. EBS for short. Specializing in arranging transportation, hotels, conference facilities and translation services for busy executives.

The venture was still at the risky stage. The three friends had sunk most of their savings into start-up costs. EBS now had an office, a small staff and a slew of international advertising. They'd landed a few jobs, but nothing big until the call from Cal Logan's executive assistant.

Turns out Logan had played football in college with one of Sabrina's old boyfriends. Said boyfriend had tipped his pal to EBS when Logan mentioned his people were scrambling to lay on a short-notice trip to Germany. Sabrina had worked twenty hours straight on the prep work and had been all set to hop a plane yesterday afternoon when the bug hit.

So here Devon was, her chin buried in a hot pink pashmina shawl, her toes frozen inside her stacked heel boots and her ears assaulted by a booming rendition of "O Tannenbaum," on her way to meet their first major client.

Again.

He'd been scheduled to arrive earlier this morning, but his assistant had called to say his corporate jet had been grounded due to icing. After considerable effort, she'd gotten him on the last commercial flight out before JFK shut down completely.

Ah, the joys of traveling this time of year! Conditions here in Dresden weren't much better. Sleet had been coming down all day. Praying her client's plane made it in before this airport closed, too, Devon hurried into the terminal.

Her breath whistled out in a sigh of relief when Logan exited Customs. She recognized him right away from the newspaper and magazine articles Sabrina had found on the Internet during her frantic prep work.

Caleb John Logan, Jr. Thirty-one. Six-two. With jet-black hair, laser blue eyes and a linebacker's shoulders under his charcoal-gray cashmere overcoat. His jaw-dropping good looks didn't score him any points with Devon, however. She'd learned the hard way not to trust handsome heartbreakers like Cal Logan.

But he was a client. An important one. And she was willing to give someone who'd served a hitch in the Marines before earning a B.S. from the University of Oregon, an MBA from Stanford and his first million at the ripe old age of twenty-six the benefit of the doubt.

Right up until he spotted the hot pink pashmina, that is.

Sabrina had indicated she'd be wearing it, and the

flash of color was certainly more visible than the sign Devon held up with his name on it. So she wasn't surprised when Logan picked her out of the crowd and cut in her direction. She'd just plastered on her best EBS smile when he whipped an arm around her waist. The next moment, she was sprawled against his cashmere-covered chest.

"Hello, Brown Eyes."

Swooping down, he covered her mouth with his.

Sheer astonishment kept Devon rooted to the spot for a few seconds while her mind whirled chaotically. Her first thought was that her client had downed a few too many drinks during the long flight. Her second, that he'd seriously mistaken the kind of escort and consulting services EBS provided. Her third shoved everything else out of her head.

Whoa, mama! The man could kiss!

His mouth moved over hers with a skill that ignited sparks at a half-dozen flash points throughout her body. Devon hadn't experienced that kind of spontaneous combustion in a while. A *long* while.

The sparks were still popping when she pushed off his chest, only now they fueled a flush of anger.

"Do you always greet women you don't know with a lip-lock, Mr. Logan?"

A smile crinkled the skin at the corners of his eyes. "As a matter of fact, I don't. That was from Don."

"Huh?"

"He said he owed you one from New Year's Eve two years ago and made me promise to deliver it."

She stared up at him in total incomprehension. Logan hooked a brow and attempted to prompt a nonexistent memory.

"He abandoned you at the Waldorf. Five minutes before midnight. To deliver twins."

"I don't have a clue who or what you're—"

Understanding burst like a water balloon.

"Wait a sec. Are you talking about Sabrina's old boyfriend? Your buddy, who's now an ob-gyn doc?"

It was Logan's turn to look startled. He recovered faster than Devon had, though. His smile widened into a rueful grin.

"I take it you're not Sabrina Russo."

"No, Mr. Logan, I am not. And if you'd listened to any of the voice mails we left on your cell phone in the past twenty-four hours," Devon added acidly, "you'd know Sabrina came down with the flu and couldn't make the trip."

"Sorry. I've been in the air for twenty-three of those twenty-four hours. I had to make a quick trip to the West Coast before turning right around and heading for Germany."

She knew that. Still, that was no excuse for his behavior. Or...what was worse...her reaction to it.

"My cell-phone battery crashed somewhere over Pennsylvania," he said, his smile holding an apology now. "I crashed somewhere over the Atlantic. Any chance we can erase what just happened and start again?"

Oh, sure. As soon as her lips stopped tingling and

her nerves snapping. Reminding herself that he was a client, Devon forced a stiff nod.

"Good." He shifted his briefcase to his left hand and held out his right. "I'm Cal Logan. And you are?"

"Devon McShay. One of Sabrina's partners."

"The history professor."

So he'd done some checking on the small firm he'd hired to work the details of his five-day, three-city swing through Germany.

"Former history professor," she corrected as she led the way toward the baggage-claim area. "I quit teaching to join forces with Sabrina and Caroline at EBS."

"Quite a career shift."

"Yes, it was."

She left it at that. No need to detail her restlessness after her divorce. Or her ex's very public, very mortifying attempt at reconciliation on the six o'clock news. Dallas hadn't been big enough for both of them after that.

That was when she'd quit her job and joined forces with her two friends. Now Devon the history prof, Sabrina the one-time party girl and Caroline the shy, quiet librarian were hard-nosed businesswomen. With pretty much the future of their fledgling enterprise hanging on how well Devon handled Cal Logan's trip.

After this rocky start, she thought grimly, things weren't looking real good.

Cal matched his stride to the staccato pace of the woman at his side. She was pissed, and no wonder.

He'd pulled some real boners in his time. This one ranked right up near the top of the list.

He'd never intended to follow through on his buddy's joking suggestion that he deliver a long-delayed New Year's Eve kiss. Then he'd exited Customs and spotted the woman he'd assumed was Sabrina Russo.

Tall and slender, with dark auburn hair caught up in a loose twist, she would have snagged any man's attention. Her high, sculpted cheekbones and the thick lashes fringing her brown eyes had certainly snagged Cal's.

Brown Eyes. Don's nickname for the woman he'd dated briefly. Except she wasn't that woman. And her eyes, Cal saw now, weren't brown. More like caramel, rich and dark, with a hint of gold in their depths.

Then there was that scarf. The hot color should have clashed with her red hair. Instead, it seemed to shout at the world to sit up and take notice.

Cal had noticed, all right. Now he'd damned well better unnotice.

Fun was fun, but he didn't need the kind of distraction Devon McShay could represent. Logan Aerospace had too much riding on the delicate negotiations that had forced him to cancel an entire week's appointments and hustle over to Germany.

"I confirmed your meeting with Herr Hauptmann for two p.m.," she informed him as suitcases began to rattle onto the baggage carousel. "I also requested early check-in at the hotel if you'd like to swing by there first."

"Definitely."

He scraped a palm across the bristles on his jaw. Given the time change, it was late morning here in Dresden but still the middle of the night U.S. time. Cal needed a shower, a shave and a full pot of coffee in him before his two o'clock meeting. As he waited for his leather carryall and suit bag to make an appearance, he gave Ms. McShay and EBS full marks for recognizing that fact.

Great start, Devon thought while her client filled out a search form for his missing luggage. *Just terrific.*

Logan had shrugged off the inconvenience with the comment that his American Express would cover the expense of delayed or lost luggage. Meanwhile Devon would have to scramble to supply him with everything from a clean shirt to pajamas.

Assuming he wore pj's. Maybe he went to bed commando. An instant, vivid image leaped into her head and refused to leap out.

Oh, for Pete's sake! She'd known the man for all of fifteen minutes and already she was imagining him naked. Disgusted, Devon tried to put the brakes on her runaway thoughts. The announcement that blared over the loudspeaker at that moment brought them to a screeching halt.

"Aufmerksamkeit, Damen und Herren."

Her head cocked, she listened as an official announced in German, English and Japanese that all flights in and out of Dresden were canceled until further notice. A chorus of groans went up inside the terminal.

By the time she escorted her client to the exit, a mile-long line of travelers was huddled in their overcoats at the taxi stand. To make matters worse, pick-up and drop-off traffic had snarled every lane. The limo Devon called on her cell phone couldn't get through the logjam.

Lord, she hated this time of year!

"The driver says he's stuck two terminals over," she related to Logan. "Traffic's not moving an inch. We can wait inside until he gets here. Or we could walk," she added with a dubious glance at the sleet still plummeting from a gunmetal-gray sky.

"I don't mind stretching my legs, but are you sure you're dressed warm enough to walk?"

"I'm fine."

Except for her boots, she admitted silently as she wove a path through the lines of frustrated travelers. Served her right for choosing style over practicality. The stacked heels and slick leather soles made for treacherous going on the icy pavement. Logan caught her as her foot almost went out from under her.

"At the risk of making an ass of myself for the second time in less than a half hour," he said solemnly, "may I suggest you hang on to me?"

Devon was only too glad to hook her elbow through his. She was also all too aware of the strength in the arm covered by layers of wool and cashmere.

He was her client. He was her client. He was her client.

She chanted the mantra over and over again as they dodged icy patches. When she finally spotted a stretch limo up ahead and confirmed it was theirs, her nose and ears tingled from the cold but Logan's solid bulk had shielded the rest of her from the worst of the knifing wind and sleet.

Devon sank into the limo's soft leather and welcome heat. Wiggling her frozen toes inside her boots, she offered Logan an apology. "I'm sorry about this hassle."

"You can't control the weather."

Or the traffic. It crawled along with the speed of a snail on Prozac. Seemingly unperturbed, Logan extracted a charger from his briefcase and plugged his cell phone into one of the limo's ports.

"Excuse me a moment while I check my calls."

He had a slew of them. The rueful glance he sent her confirmed that several were from EBS. He was still on the phone when the limo finally reached the airport exit. The slick roads made Devon grateful for the fact that Sabrina had somehow managed to wrangle last-minute reservations at the Westin Hotel across the river from the oldest part of Dresden. With any luck, efficient road crews would have the roads sanded before she and Logan had to tackle the Old City's maze of narrow, cobbled streets.

Devon had checked into the hotel yesterday afternoon and sunk like a stone into its heavenly feather bed. Hopefully, Cal Logan would decide on a power nap and do the same while she hit the shops for whatever he would need. She led the way through a lobby decorated with fragrant pine boughs and skirted a twenty-foot Christmas tree, only to have the desk clerk send her hopes crashing.

"I'm very sorry, Ms. McShay. The guest presently occupying Mr. Logan's suite hasn't yet departed."

"But you indicated there would be no problem with early check-in."

"I didn't think there would be, madam. Unfortunately, the present occupant's flight has been canceled, and he's requested a late checkout pending other arrangements."

"How late?"

"He's one of our platinum customers," the clerk said with a look that pleaded for understanding. "We have to give him until four o'clock."

Smothering an extremely unprofessional curse, Devon turned to her client. Logan had shrugged off the irritating glitches so far, but the crease between his brows suggested his patience was stretching thin.

Hastily, she dug in her purse for the key card to her room. It wasn't a VIP suite, but it did have a spacious sitting room, a separate bedroom and that incredible down comforter.

"Why don't you go up to my room and relax?" she said with determined cheerfulness. "You can give me a list of what you'll need until your luggage gets here, and I'll hit the shops."

If his luggage got here. Judging by his clipped response, Logan considered the possibility as remote as she did.

"All I need right now is a shirt that doesn't look like it's been slept in. White or blue. Neck, sixteen and a half, sleeves thirty-two."

Whatever that translated to in German. Devon had enjoyed several mild flirtations and one serious fling during her year at the University of Salzburg but hadn't gotten around to purchasing men's clothing. Sternly, she banished visions of sending Logan into his meeting with Herr Hauptmann wearing a shirt with a collar that choked him or cuffs that dangled well below his suit coat sleeves.

"White or blue," she repeated. "Sixteen and a half. Thirty-two. Got it."

Summoning a breezy smile, she handed him the key.

"It's room four-twelve. I need a few things, too. I'll look around the shops for a couple of hours. Stretch out and make yourself comfortable, Mr. Logan. I'll buzz the room before I come up."

His incipient frown eased. "We're going to be spending the next five days together. Please, call me Cal."

Devon hesitated. She and Sabrina and Caroline had all agreed they needed to maintain a strictly professional relationship with their clients. Especially ones as powerful and influential as Caleb John Logan, Jr.

On the other hand, he *was* the client. Refusing his

request wasn't really an option after the annoying glitches they'd encountered so far.

"Cal it is. See you in a few hours."

She dragged out the shopping as long as she could and dawdled over coffee in the lobby café until close to twelve-thirty. Just to be on the safe side, she called Herr Hauptmann's office to confirm the meeting was still on for two o'clock before searching out a house phone. Her client answered on the second ring.

"Logan."

"I'm sorry to wake you, but we'll need to leave soon."

"No problem. I've been crunching numbers."

"I have your shirt."

"Great, bring it up."

As the elevator whisked upward with noiseless efficiency, Devon's thoughts whirled. She'd ordered the limo for one. Hopefully the roads would be sanded and relatively clear. She'd better arrange backup transportation to Berlin tomorrow, too, just in case the airport was still shut down. She'd check the high-speed train schedules, she decided as she rapped on her room door, and...

When the door opened, her thoughts skittered to a dead stop. Cal Logan in cashmere and worsted wool could make any woman whip around for another look. Shirtless and bare-chested, he'd give a post-menopausal nun heart palpitations.

Two

As their limo crossed the centuries-old stone bridge leading into Dresden's Old City, Devon was still trying to recover. She couldn't remember the last time she'd gotten up close and personal with that much naked chest.

"What's going on?"

Logan's question banished her mental image of taut, contoured pecs and a dusting of black hair that arrowed downward. Blinking, she saw him lean forward to survey the town square just across the bridge.

It was one of the most beautiful in all Europe. Although almost eighty percent of Dresden had been destroyed during two days of intense bombing in World War Two, decades of meticulous restoration had resurrected much of the city's glorious architecture. The monumental Baroque cathedral with its openwork dome tower dominated a three-block area that included a royal palace, a magnificent state opera house and the world-famous Zwinger, a collection of incredibly ornate buildings surrounding a massive courtyard once used to stage tournaments and festivals.

It wasn't the architecture that had captured Cal Logan's attention, though, but the outdoor market in full swing despite the miserable weather. Shoppers bundled in down jackets, ski masks, stocking caps and earmuffs roamed rows of wooden stalls crammed with handicrafts.

"It's a *Christkindlmarkt,*" Devon told him. "A Christmas market. Most towns and cities in Germany have one. The tradition dates back to the early 1400s, when regular seasonal markets took place throughout the year. The Christmas market evolved into *the* major event, where locals would gather to sell homemade toys, ornaments and foodstuffs."

Thus initiating the commercialization process that had expanded over the years to its present mania. As a historian, Devon admired the medieval atmosphere of this lively town square. The self-proclaimed Grinchette in her had to work to see past the throngs of eager shoppers.

"Dresden's market is one of the oldest in Germany. And that—" her nod indicated the wooden structure dominating the square "—is the tallest Christmas pyramid in the world."

Most traditional, multitiered wooden Christmas pyramids were tabletop size. Carved figures depicting the Nativity decorated each of the tiers. Candles sat in holders at the pyramid's base. When the candles were lit, warm air rose and turned the propeller-style fan at the top, causing the various tiers to rotate.

What had begun as traditional folk art designed to delight children with the dancing shadows cast by the rotating figures was now a multimillion-dollar industry. Wooden Christmas pyramids were sold all over the world, and less expensive versions were machine cut instead of hand carved. Dresden, however, had taken the traditional concept to new and ridiculous heights.

Okay, maybe not so ridiculous. As the limo inched along the jam-packed street leading past the market, Devon had to concede the fifty-foot pyramid with its life-size figures was a pretty awesome sight.

Cal Logan evidently thought so, too. He twisted around for another glimpse of the busy square.

"I'd like to hit some of those stalls after the meeting with Herr Hauptmann." He settled back in his seat and caught her surprised expression. "I have nine nieces and nephews," he explained.

Nine? Devon made a mental adjustment to reconcile Cal Logan's public image as a jet-setting playboy with that of a doting uncle.

"How old are they?"

"Beats me. The littlest one is…little. The oldest just started high school. I think."

So much for the doting uncle!

"You'll need a better fix on their ages if you plan to shop for Christmas gifts."

"My executive assistant usually takes care of that," Logan admitted. "She'll have names, ages and personal preferences in her computer."

Devon got the hint. A quick glance at her watch confirmed it was still early back at Logan Aerospace corporate headquarters in eastern Connecticut. She'd bet the boss's executive assistant would be one of the first ones in, though. Luckily, Devon had added the woman's phone number and e-mail to her personal-contacts list.

"I'll e-mail her," she said, digging in her purse for her iPhone. "By the time we get out of the meeting with Herr Hauptmann, she should be at work and have access to the information."

With something less than enthusiasm, Devon worked the iPhone's tiny keyboard. She'd counted on this trip to provide an escape from the shopping frenzy back home. Now she'd have to brave the nasty weather and wade into a mob of shoppers to help her client find gifts for a whole pack of nieces and nephews. Thank goodness she'd had enough experience with German and Austrian winters to have worn her warmest coat.

Hauptmann Metal Works was located southeast of the Old City, in a section of Dresden that had been reconstructed along depressingly modern lines.

Remnants of East Germany's long domination by the Soviet Union showed in seemingly endless rows of concrete-block buildings. Some attempts had been made to soften their stark utilitarianism with newly planted parks and pastel color schemes, but the area held none of the old-world charm of other parts of the city.

Herr Hauptmann was awaiting their arrival. Big and beefy and ruddy cheeked, the German industrialist came out of his office to greet them. Devon had confirmed that he spoke fluent English, so she wasn't required to translate as he shook hands with his visitor.

"Welcome, Herr Logan. I have been looking forward to meeting you."

"Thank you, sir. This is Ms. Devon McShay. She's assisting me during my visit to Germany."

"Ms. McShay."

Devon had intended to make sure her client had everything he needed before fading into the woodwork with the other underlings, but Logan ushered her to a seat beside his at the long conference table.

Ten minutes of chitchat and a welcoming toast of schnapps later, she had plunged feet first into the world of high finance. The numbers Logan and Hauptmann lobbed back and forth like tennis balls left her breathless. They weren't talking millions, but billions.

The main issue centered on the massive, joint-European venture to build the Airbus, touted as the world's biggest passenger jet. A number of American companies were involved in it as well, including Logan Aerospace. Devon had to struggle to follow the discussion of the incredibly complex global aerospace industry. She grasped the bottom line, though, when Logan leaned forward an hour later and summed it up with surgical precision.

"We can argue the numbers all day, Herr Hauptmann, but we both agree your company is dangerously overleveraged. You borrowed heavily to hire additional people and invest in new production facilities to win your big Airbus contract. With Airbus behind schedule and facing major cost overruns, its potential customers are dropping like flies. You can go down with them, or you can accept my offer of a buyout, which will not only save your Airbus contracts, it will give you greater access to American aerospace giants like Boeing and Lockheed."

"At a significantly reduced profit margin."

"For the first three years, until we've recouped your investment outlay."

The tension in the conference room was almost palpable.

"This company has been in my family for four generations, Herr Logan. It goes very much against my grain to relinquish control of it."

Devon held her breath as the two men faced each other across the conference table. She saw no trace of the even-tempered client who'd shrugged off the irritations of travel delays and lost luggage in the steely eyed corporate raider who went straight for the jugular.

"You've already lost control, sir."

Hauptmann's ruddy cheeks took on an even darker hue. Devon gulped, hoping he didn't have a stroke as Logan delivered the coup de grace.

"I know you've had a similar offer from one of my competitors, Templeton Systems. I don't know the terms, of course, but I do know Templeton's standard practice is to replace key managers at every level with their own people."

The other executives present shifted uncomfortably in their seats. Logan swept a glance around the table before meeting their boss's gaze again.

"I'm willing to work with you on a restructuring plan that will mesh the skills of your people with any of my own I decide to put in place."

All eyes shifted to Hauptmann. Frowning, he worked his mouth from side to side for several moments.

"How long is this offer on the table?" he asked finally.

"I leave Dresden tomorrow for Berlin to finalize the financial arrangements. Then I plan to make a quick visit to the Airbus production plant in Hamburg before I fly back to the States on Friday. I'll need your answer by then."

"Very well. You shall have it."

Wow! These guys played hardball. Five days to make a multibillion-dollar decision. Devon was impressed.

With a visible effort, Hauptmann shelved his

company's fate and played the gracious host. "What a shame you have only one night in our beautiful city. Our Boys' Choir is giving a special Christmas performance at the opera house tonight. My wife and I would very much like for you to join us for the concert and a late dinner. And your lovely assistant, of course."

Devon fully expected Logan to make a polite excuse. He'd been traveling for twenty-plus hours and had spent the brief respite in her room prepping for this meeting. Surely he wanted to crash.

Or not.

Showing no sign of the fatigue he must be feeling, Logan accepted the invitation.

"Excellent." Hauptmann pumped his hand again and escorted him out of the office. "I'll send a driver to pick you up at your hotel at seven."

Devon waited until they were outside and in the limo to release a long breath. "Whew! That was pretty amazing. My father's an accountant, so I'm used to hearing him throw around numbers. Never any as big as those, though. Do you think Herr Hauptmann will accept your offer?"

"We'll know by Friday."

He was so nonchalant about it. If she hadn't just seen him going in for the kill, she might not have believed all those news articles Sabrina had found on the Web citing his lethal skills as a corporate raider.

"Do you still want to stop at the Christmas market?"

"If we have time."

It was almost four now. They would have to hustle to hit the jam-packed market, select gifts for an assortment of kids, check on Logan's luggage and get him moved into his suite in time to shower and change. Maybe, she thought hopefully, his executive assistant had decided to take the morning off and hadn't responded to Devon's e-mail requesting the names, ages and gift preferences of Logan's nieces and nephews.

No such luck. The response was waiting when she clicked on her iPhone. She scrolled through the list once and was going over it a second time when their limo slowed for the crowded streets of the Old City. Devon caught a glimpse of the market through a narrow alleyway. They could sit in the car while it crawled another quarter mile to the square or cut through the alley and meet the limo on the other side.

"Hier ist gut," she told the driver.

He pulled over to the curb and his passengers climbed out. The sleet had let up a little, thank goodness, but the air was still cold enough to make her teeth ache.

"I'll tell the driver to wait for us by the bridge, Mr.… Er… Cal."

He eyed her coat and the hot pink shawl she draped over her head and wrapped around the lower half of her face. "You sure you'll be warm enough? We can skip the market and go straight back to the hotel."

Devon was tempted to take the out he offered. *Very* tempted. All she had to do was fake one little shiver. But they were out of the limo now, and the market was only a short walk away.

"I'm good if you are."

Nodding, he hiked up the collar of his overcoat and pulled a pair of gloves from his pocket. When they started down the cobblestone alley, he took her elbow with same courtesy he had at the airport.

Devon wasn't sure how such a simple gesture could be so casually polite and so damned disconcerting at the same time. She made a conscious effort not to lean into his warmth as their heels echoed on the ancient stones.

The narrow walk wound around the back of the great cathedral. Thankfully, the cathedral walls blocked most of the wind. The gusts that did whistle through the alley, however, carried tantalizing scents. Devon's nose twitched at the aroma of hot chocolate, apple cider spiced with cinnamon and cloves, freshly baked gingerbread and the sticky sweet cake Dresden was so famous for.

"You'll have to try the stollen," she told her client. "It's a German specialty that's supposed to have originated right here in Dresden."

Sure enough, when they exited the alley and joined the throng in the main square, the first booth they encountered was selling slices of the cake still warm and steaming from the oven.

"When in Rome…"

Taking her at her word, Logan steered her toward the line at the booth.

Not Logan. Cal. Still struggling to make the mental adjustment, Devon dredged her memory bank for details of the treat so popular throughout Germany and Austria.

"The Catholic Church used to forbid the consumption of butter as part of the fasting in preparation for Christmas. Sometime in the sixteenth century, the Elector of Saxony got permission from the Pope for his baker's guild to use butter and milk when baking their Christmas bread. Dresden's stollen became highly prized after that, and every year the baker's guild would march through the streets to present the first, huge loaf to the prince in gratitude."

She could imagine the color and pageantry of that medieval processional, with trumpets sounding and the bakers in all their finery tromping through the snow with their thirty-six pound loaves. The tradition still continued, she knew, only now it was a mega-parade complete with floats, marching bands, a stollen queen and a five-ton loaf!

"Here you go."

Logan—*Cal*—passed her a paper-wrapped slice and a foam cup of something hot and steamy. He retrieved the same for himself before they lucked out and found space at one of the stand-up tables dotting the square.

Devon's first bite more than made up for the cold nipping at her cheeks and nose. Eyes closed in ecstasy, she savored the rich blend of nuts, raisins, candied fruits flavored with spices and brandy and, of course, tablespoons of butter.

The hot chocolate was also spiked, she discovered after the first sip. As a result, she was feeling warm both inside and out when they dumped their trash in a handy container.

"Ready to do some serious stall hopping?" she asked.

"Hang on. You've got powdered sugar on your lip."

He moved closer, and for a startled moment Devon thought he was going to repeat his performance at the airport and kiss away the sugar. Her heart speeded up, and she didn't know whether she was more relieved or disappointed when he tugged off a glove and brushed his thumb along her lip.

Then she looked up and caught the lazy half smile in his eyes. For the most absurd moment, the cold and the crowd seemed to fade away. She held her breath as his thumb made another pass. Warm. Slow. Caressing.

"There." He dropped his arm. "All clear."

With the brandy heating her stomach and his touch searing her skin, the best Devon could manage was a gruff "Thanks."

Sweating a little under her heavy wool coat, she edged her way into the crowd that snaked through lanes of brightly decorated stalls. Thanks to her client's efficient assistant, picking out gifts took little effort.

Four-year-old Andrew got a hand-carved train on wooden tracks. Seven-year old Jason scored a two-foot-tall nutcracker in a smart red coat. For the twins,

Julia and Bethany, Devon recommended denim skirts lavishly trimmed with filigree lace from Plauen. The more studious Janet received a glass globe of the world handblown and painted by a local artisan, while baby Nick got mittens and a stocking cap in a downy yarn that sparkled like spun gold.

Dusk was falling and the strings of lights illuminating the market had popped on by the time Cal and Devon rounded out the purchases with a doll in a fur-trimmed red dress, a wooden puppet and a chess set featuring incredibly detailed Prussian soldiers. Their arms full, they had started for the bridge and the waiting limo when a ripple of eager anticipation raced through the crowd. They turned just in time see the giant fir next to the wooden Christmas pyramid light up.

A chorus of collective ooooohs filled the square. It was followed by the sound of young voices raised in a joyous rendition of "O Tannenbaum."

Second time today, Devon thought. Strangely, though, the song didn't produce quite the same level of cynicism as when she'd heard it blasting through the loudspeakers at the airport.

Maybe because these voices were so young and angelic, or because she still felt the glow from the spiked hot chocolate. Certainly *not* because her lip still tingled from Cal Logan's touch.

"There's the car."

The driver had pulled into a cul-de-sac beside the bridge spanning the Elbe and was sitting with the engine idling. He jumped out to relieve them of their packages, but the magical view drew his passengers to the wall fronting the river's bank. Completely enchanted, Devon leaned both hands on the wall.

The ancient stone bridge spanned the Elbe in a series of graceful arches. Below the bridge, the river was a solid sheet of dark, glistening ice. Atop it, the statues of saints and kings along both sides had acquired a coating of frost that glittered in the glow of the street lamps, while the trees lining both banks were strung with white lights that turned the icy nightscape into a winter wonderland.

"Now that," Devon murmured, "is a sight."

Cal shifted his gaze to his companion's profile. The instant attraction that had prompted him to make a fool of himself at the airport this morning returned with a swift and unexpected kick.

"Yes," he agreed, "it is."

Interesting what a difference a few hours could make, he mused as he leaned an elbow on the cold stone of the wall. He'd arrived in Germany intent on acquiring a subsidiary that would cost him billions but make Logan Aerospace one of the top U.S. players in the European market.

He was still determined to acquire Hauptmann Metal Works. Betting on the outcome, he'd finalize the financial details when he met with his bankers in Berlin tomorrow. But the heat that stirred in his belly as his gaze lingered on Devon McShay was fast convincing him he should acquire her as well.

Three

"Logan kissed you?"

The question shot from Devon's two partners almost simultaneously. She nodded in response, wondering how the world had survived before digital videoconferencing.

"He did."

Her partners' images filled her laptop's split screen. She'd caught Sabrina at home, still flushed and feverish but on the road to recovery. Caroline was at the office. Devon knew without being told she'd been up since dawn and hard at it.

The two women couldn't have been more different. Sabrina Russo came from a privileged background and had partied her way through college.

Caroline Walters was quiet and withdrawn and had worked part-time jobs to earn spending money even during their shared year at the university. At this moment, however, their faces wore almost identical expressions of surprise.

"Logan thought I was you, Sabrina."

"Huh?"

"That was pretty much my reaction, too."

Swiftly, Devon explained about the long-delayed New Year's Eve kiss.

"That sounds like Don Howard." The blonde shook her head in mingled amusement and exasperation. "So how did you handle it?"

"I didn't slug our client on the spot," Devon drawled, "but I came close."

After she'd recovered from her near total meltdown, that is. She couldn't explain the ridiculous reaction to herself, let alone her partners. Nor did she mention the way her nerves tingled every time Logan took her arm. Shelving her completely irrational sensitivity to the man's touch, she ran through the string of disasters that had begun with his long-delayed flight and ended just minutes ago, when she finally moved him into his suite.

"At least I got him to his meeting with Herr Hauptmann on time. Believe it or not," she added with a grimace, "at Cal's request we also squeezed in some post-meeting Christmas shopping."

"Uh-oh."

Instant sympathy filled Caroline's forest green

eyes. She knew how this time of year scratched at Devon's old wounds. Sabrina had zoned in on another aspect of her comment, however.

"Cal?" she echoed.

"He insists we proceed on a first-name basis."

Devon glanced at her bedroom window. She hadn't even had time to draw the drapes before she dashed into the bathroom to freshen her makeup and change. Ordinarily, she would have found the illuminated spires across the river magical. Their coat of glistening ice instilled a less enthusiastic response tonight.

"On the negative side," she told her partners, "there's still no sign of his luggage, and the weather reports are grim. Everything's shutting down. The airport, the trains, the autobahn. We may be stuck in Dresden indefinitely."

"Logan can't hold you responsible for the weather," Caroline protested.

"Or EBS," Sabrina added briskly. Despite the party-girl persona she projected to the rest of the world, she was the partner with the most business sense. Only Devon and Caroline knew the personal hell she'd gone through to gain that knowledge.

"Has he made any noises about being dissatisfied with EBS's services?" she wanted to know.

"No complaints so far. That could change real fast, though. Between getting ready for this concert and dinner tonight and giving you guys an update, I didn't have time to work backup transportation and hotel reservations."

Caroline jumped in, as Devon had hoped she would. "I'll take care of that. We've got Logan's schedule and current itinerary on the computer. I'll work up a list of alternative options and have them waiting for you when you get back from the concert."

"Thanks, Caro. I didn't plan on an evening out."

"Good thing I talked you into packing your long velvet skirt."

That came from Sabrina, who firmly believed appearance and flexibility were as important in their business as organizational skills. All three were getting a real test tonight.

"What are you wearing with it?"

"The gold lamé number you also made me pack."

Devon leaned away from the computer's built-in camera to display the scoop-necked, cap-sleeved top in glittering gold. Lightweight and silky, it could jazz up a suit for an after-five cocktail meeting or provide an elegant stand-alone for an evening function like this.

"Perfect," Sabrina announced. "Now go eat, don't drink and be merry."

"Yes, ma'am."

Cal escorted her to the lobby and the car Herr Hauptmann had sent. His hair was still damp from his shower and the tangy lemon-lime scent of his aftershave teased her senses.

The two-hour concert provided another banquet for her senses. Dresden's opera house had been leveled during World War Two and damaged again when the Elbe flooded its banks in 2002. But huge infusions of funds had restored the theater to its former glory. Pale green walls, magnificent ceiling paintings and the ornate molding on its tiers of boxes made an incredible backdrop for the Dresden Boys' Choir. The ensemble rivaled Vienna's for the purity of the voices. The singers' notes soared high, sounding as though they flew on angels' wings

Dinner afterward was smaller and more intimate but every bit as elegant. Herr Hauptmann had reserved a corner table at Das Caroussel, located in a recently restored Baroque palace. Mindful of Sabrina's parting advice, Devon feasted on braised veal accompanied by a sauerbraten ravioli that made her taste buds want to weep with joy, but limited her alcohol intake to a few sips of a light, fruity Rhine wine.

Madam Hauptmann was a surprise. Vivacious and petite next to her husband's bulk, she spoke flawless English and was delighted to learn Devon had studied in her native Austria. She was also *very* impressed with Cal Logan. As dinner progressed and the waiter refilled her wine glass, Lisel Hauptmann's playful flirtation began to include seemingly accidental touches and sidelong glances her husband failed to note.

Devon noticed them, however. The beauty of the concert and the luxurious restaurant evaporated bit by bit. By the time coffee was served, her dessert of Jerusalem pear and artichoke vinaigrette tasted more like chalk with every bite.

She'd had to endure countless scenes like this during her short-lived marriage to Blake McShay. Tall and trim and salon-tanned, her husband had played his flamboyant good looks and TV-personality role for all they were worth. But only for PR purposes, or so Blake would argue when Devon objected to the way he let women fawn all over him.

To Cal Logan's credit, he appeared completely oblivious to Madam Hauptmann's less-than-subtle signals. That should have won him some brownie points with Devon, but the bad taste stayed with her after the Hauptmanns dropped them off at their hotel. She returned short, noncommittal responses to her client's comments during the walk through the lobby and said even less in the elevator.

The plush, patterned carpet lining the hall muted their footsteps as they approached Cal's suite. He stopped beside the double doors but didn't insert the key. Tapping the key card against his hand, he raked a glance over her face.

"You okay?"

"I'm fine," she lied.

In fact, she was anything but. Watching Lisel Hauptmann's performance had stirred too many nasty memories. All Devon wanted was to crawl between the sheets and let sleep wipe them away. Her client's long day gave her the perfect out.

"But you must be exhausted," she said. "I'll check the weather and call you in a few minutes with our revised itinerary for tomorrow."

"Why don't you bring me a printed copy? We can have a cognac while we go over the details."

"I don't care for cognac."

He cocked a brow at the stiff response. "I'm sure we can fine something else to suit your tastes. See you in a few minutes."

"Fine."

Devon could feel those blue eyes drilling into her back as she marched the few yards to her room and knew she had to get a grip here.

So Cal Logan was too damned hot for his own— or anyone else's—good? So he and this crazy time of year combined to throw her off balance? She'd darn well better get her head on straight before she trotted back to the man's suite.

The e-mail from Caroline didn't help in that regard. Her heart sinking, Devon skimmed the meager contents. European weather experts had already labeled this the ice storm of the century. Many airports had closed until further notice. Trains were running hours behind schedule, if at all. Road conditions were expected to worsen overnight. The experts predicted widespread power outages as trees groaning with the weight of ice cracked and toppled electrical lines.

Caroline's advice was to hunker down right where they were and wait out the storm. With great reluctance, Devon called down to the desk to check on room availability should they have to extend.

"It should not be a problem, madam."

Ha! She'd heard that before.

"If you and Herr Logan cannot depart because of this storm, our other guests most likely cannot arrive. In either case, we will work out suitable arrangements."

Vowing to hold them to that promise, Devon printed the e-mail and headed back down the hall.

"It's not looking good for travel to Berlin tomorrow," she announced when Cal opened the door.

"I heard."

Ushering her inside, he gestured to the plasma TV mounted on the wall. The screen showed a scene of almost eerie beauty. Like slender, long-limbed ballerinas, a row of ice-coated linden trees bowed almost to the ground.

"I caught the tail end of a CNN Europe broadcast. Evidently this front isn't expected to move any time soon. We need to discuss options."

He'd shed his suit coat and loosened his tie. He'd also popped the top buttons of his blue shirt and rolled up the cuffs. As he reached for the doors of the highboy that housed the suite's well-stocked bar, Devon caught the gleam of a thin gold watch on his wrist, all the more noticeable against skin tanned to dark oak.

It was a deep, natural color that couldn't have come from a bottle or the cocoon of a tanning bed. Devon should know. Her ex had spent megabucks on the latter. And those white squint lines at the corners of his eyes weren't the result of peering at spreadsheets. Cal Logan might run a corporation that employed thousands, but he didn't do it exclusively from the confines of a corner office.

"You said you're not a cognac devotee. What would you like?"

The dazzling array of bottles beckoned. She'd been careful to take only a taste of schnapps during the welcome toasts at Herr Hauptmann's office and a few sips of wine at dinner. With her client's trip coming apart at the seams, though, she decided on a shot of something stronger than the diet Sprite she started to ask for.

"Baileys would be good. On the rocks."

"One Baileys coming up."

While he splashed the creamy liqueur into a brandy snifter, Devon took a quick glance around. Since the suite's previous occupant had delayed his checkout, she hadn't been able to inspect it before Cal moved in. She needn't have worried. From what she could see, the King's Suite more than lived up to the hotel's proud claim that royalty had slept here, not to mention presidents, prime ministers and a good number of rock stars.

The luxurious apartment consisted of four rooms, each filled with what looked like priceless antiques. In the sitting room, gas-fed flames flickered in a marble fireplace with a mantel so ornate she guessed it had once graced a prince's palace. The adjacent dining area boasted gilt-edged wainscoting and a chandelier dripping crystal teardrops. Separate bedrooms flanked the two central rooms.

Through the open double doors of one, Devon caught a glimpse of a stunning headboard carved with hunting scenes and topped by a life-size wooden stag's head. Pale gold brocade covered the walls of the second bedroom. Bed curtains in the same shimmering silk were draped from the crown-shaped medallion centered above a magnificent four-poster.

"Wow," Devon murmured. "I've toured castles that weren't as richly appointed."

"Me, too." Cal came to stand beside her. Amusement laced his voice as he surveyed the decadent splendor. "Kind of makes you wonder what went on behind those bed curtains on cold, dark nights like this one."

Devon's back stiffened. She sent him a sharp glance, but there was nothing suggestive in the look he turned her way.

Or was there?

She was still trying to interpret his lazy half smile when he handed her the Baileys and retrieved his snifter of cognac from the marble-topped coffee table. With a ping of crystal on crystal, he tipped his glass to hers.

"Here's to Mother Nature. For better or worse, she's calling the shots."

"For the foreseeable future, anyway."

Devon lifted the snifter to her lips. Her first sip of the cool, creamy liqueur went down like a chocolate milkshake. The second hit with a little more punch.

"I called the front desk," she told Cal as she moved toward the high-backed sofa angled to face the fire. "If necessary, we can hole up here until the storm breaks."

His gaze went to the sitting-room windows. The drapes were drawn back to showcase Old City's illuminated spires and turrets. The sleet blurring the world-famous view gave it an impressionistic, almost surreal, quality.

"Looks like holing up is becoming more necessary by the moment."

Devon had to agree. "I'll call the people you were supposed to meet with in Berlin and Hamburg first thing in the morning and try to reschedule. Do you have any flexibility in when you need to return to the States?"

"I would prefer not to spend Christmas Day in Germany. Or in the air," he added with a wry smile. "As the only non-dad in the family, my sisters usually make me play Santa for my nieces and nephews."

"Beard and all?"

"Beard and all." He sank into the cushions at the other end of the sofa and stretched his feet toward the fire. "I'd hate to miss Christmas with my family and certainly wouldn't want to deprive you of being with yours."

"Not a problem for me."

Evidently Devon's shrug didn't come across as careless as she'd intended. Cal eyes held a question as he regarded her from a few feet away.

"No close family?"

"No brothers or sisters, and my parents divorced when I was a kid," she explained. "It wasn't an amicable parting of the ways."

To say the least. Devon hid a grimace behind a swallow of smooth, chocolaty liqueur.

"They fought over where I'd spend every holiday and vacation. I got so I dreaded school breaks."

"The fighting hasn't let up now that you're an adult?"

"If anything, it's worse. Now they lay the decision on me, along with the guilt. That's one of the reasons I was more than happy to step in and take this trip when Sabrina got hit with the flu."

"What about someone else?" Cal asked casually. "Someone special to catch under the mistletoe?"

Devon squirmed, remembering Blake's proposal under that damned sprig of green. No way she intended to relate the fiasco that had followed. Or her ridiculous, starry-eyed belief she'd finally broken the Christmas curse.

"No one special."

"Good."

"Excuse me?"

"I've been wondering about that since you picked me up at the airport this morning."

Calmly, he set his brandy snifter on the coffee table, reached across the cushions and removed hers from her hand. Devon went from surprised to instantly wary as he laid his arm across the back of the sofa.

"I've also been wondering if that kiss hit you with the same wallop it did me."

Oh, boy! Where had that come from? Hastily, Devon scrambled to get things back on a less personal basis.

"How it hit either of us is completely irrelevant, Mr. Logan."

"Cal."

"This is a business trip, *Mr.* Logan. For me as well as you."

"We took care of business this afternoon. Even hard-charging professionals are entitled to some downtime."

"*You* took care of business this afternoon. I'm still on duty."

His mouth curving, he rendered a snappy salute that reminded her that this sophisticated multibillionaire had once been a lowly private or lieutenant or whatever.

"Now hear this," he intoned. "This is your captain speaking. All hands are officially at liberty."

"It doesn't work like that," she said stubbornly.

"Sure it does. So answer the question, McShay. Did you feel the same kick I did?"

Every shred of common sense Devon possessed shrieked at her to lie like hell. Despite his blithe assurances to the contrary, her gut told her she should *not* mix business and pleasure. Especially with someone like Cal Logan. He was too powerful, too charismatic. Too damned sexy.

On the other hand...

Stop right there! There *was* no other hand. She'd been burned once by a handsome, charismatic charmer. She'd be a fool to stick her hand in the fire again.

"I repeat, Mr. Logan, how it hit either of us is completely irrelevant. I don't intend to—"

She broke off, blinking as the cityscape that had filled the windows behind Cal suddenly went black. Dresden's beautiful spires and turrets disappeared before her eyes. In almost the next second, the luxurious King's Suite plunged into darkness broken only by the flames leaping in the marble fireplace.

Four

"A major substation went down."

Cal hung up the house phone and confirmed what he and Devon already suspected.

"Power is gone to half the city, with more outages being reported as we speak."

The flickering flames from the fireplace painted his face in shades of bronze as he crossed the room. His shadow loomed large against the pale walls.

"The desk clerk says the hotel has a backup generator, but…"

Devon's heart sank. She had a feeling the "but" was a lead-in to something she didn't want to hear. Sure enough, Cal delivered the grim news.

"It provides only enough power for emergency-exit lighting."

Leaving the rest of the hotel in the dark.

"How long do they think the power will be out?"

"They have no idea. They're hoping it'll just be a few hours."

Terrific! What better way to end a day characterized by more screwups and miscues than she wanted to count? Suddenly weary beyond words, Devon ached to sink into her featherbed and sleep right through this latest disaster.

"I think we should pack it in," she suggested. "There's nothing more we can do tonight."

Cal accompanied her to the door but leaned an elbow against the ornate molding. "Actually, there is. You could answer my question. Did you feel the same punch I did?"

As if she was going to admit he'd rocked her back on her heels at the airport this morning!

"I don't intend to answer it," she said primly.

"Coward."

The soft taunt held as much amusement as speculation. Devon responded to both with a lift of her chin.

"The kiss was a mistake. Or more correctly, a case of mistaken identity. Your friend asked you deliver it to someone he no doubt described as a good-time girl."

Which Sabrina Russo most definitely had been. Only Devon and Caroline knew how hard their friend had to work now to maintain her laughing, effervescent facade.

"In case you haven't noticed," Devon said coolly, "I'm not that woman."

"Trust me, I've noticed."

This far from the fire, the room was in deep shadow. She couldn't read Cal's expression, but the amusement was still there, lacing his deep voice.

"So here's the deal," he said. "I'm thinking we should try it again."

"What?"

"No mistakes or mistaken identities. Just you and me this time. We'll test the waters, see if we experience the same punch."

Devon gave an exasperated huff. Despite her every effort to maintain a businesslike attitude, her client wasn't going to let go of that ridiculous incident at the airport unless and until she killed it stone-cold dead.

Assuming she could. With him leaning over her, his features a contrast of light and dark, she had the mortifying suspicion she could lose herself in Cal Logan's arms.

The mere thought tightened the muscles low in her belly. For a dangerous moment, she indulged the fantasy of popping the rest of his shirt buttons. Sliding her palms over the contours of his chest. Locking her arms around the strong column of his neck.

Summoning every ounce of willpower she possessed, Devon wrapped her hand around the gilt-trimmed latch and yanked the door open.

"Good night, *Mr.* Logan."

* * *

Cal let her go. He'd heard the rusty edge of exhaustion layered under the irritation in her voice. She had to feel almost as whipped as he did.

He knew damned well his tiredness would have evaporated on the spot if she'd taken him up on his challenge. But would hers? His rapidly evolving plans for Devon McShay didn't include a sleepy, halfhearted seduction. He wanted her wide awake, her breath coming in short gasps, her body eager and straining against his.

Cal scraped a hand across his chin, trying to remember the last time a woman had roused this kind of hunger in him, this fast. From the first glimpse, Devon had stirred his interest. From the first taste, she'd dominated his thoughts. All during the meeting with Hauptmann, Cal had had to work to keep his attention on the acquisition details and off the woman sitting next to him.

He was damned if he understood why. Even with Alexis—beautiful, sensual, avaricious Alexis—a part of him had always remained detached. And more than a little cynical. He'd known from day one that the glamorous blonde had been more attracted to his millions than to him.

Yet prickly, stubborn Devon, who insisted on maintaining a professional distance, had Cal plotting all kinds of devious ways to get her in his bed. He had several in mind as he crossed the darkened room, intending to toss down the rest of his cognac before he hit the sheets. A sharp rap brought him back to the door.

When he opened it, his pulse spiked. Devon stood in the hall. For a wild moment, Cal was sure she'd come back to conduct the experiment he'd suggested.

"The key to my room doesn't work."

So much for his misguided hopes, he thought wryly.

"I used the house phone to call the front desk. They think the sudden power outage sent a jolt through the computer that electronically resets the hotel's door locks."

The only lighting came via the red emergency-exit signs. It was more than enough for Cal to note her thoroughly disgusted expression.

"Until they get the computer back online, not even security or housekeeping can let me in. So I thought… Since you have two bedrooms… Maybe we could…"

"Share?"

"Yes."

"Sure. Come in."

He stood aside, careful to keep his expression neutral as she swept by him. She was clearly upset by this latest turn of events. That didn't stop him from feeling a whole lot like the big bad wolf when Red Riding Hood appeared with her basket of goodies.

She halted in the sitting room, her slender figure silhouetted against the glow from the fireplace. "Which bedroom are you using?"

He gestured to the one on the right. "I went for the stag's head instead of the crown."

"Okay." She hesitated. "Well, uh, I guess I'll turn in."

He had to fight a grin. He shouldn't be enjoying her predicament so much. "'Night, Devon. I'll see you in the morning."

"Good night."

He waited to see if she'd tack on another *Mr.* Logan. She didn't.

When the door closed behind her, a fierce satisfaction gripped Cal. He was halfway home. He had Devon here, in his lair. That was progress enough for tonight.

Or so he thought.

An hour later he was forced to admit he'd made a serious error in judgment. With the electric heat out, the room temperatures had gone down like the *Titanic*. The thick comforter provided sufficient protection against the cold, but all Cal could think of was how much warmer he'd be with Devon curled up beside him. The fact that she slept less than a dozen yards away kept him awake and aching long into the cold, dark night.

Devon woke to sunlight so bright and dazzling she had to put up an arm to shield her eyes. Squinting through her elbow, she saw she'd neglected to draw the pale gold brocade drapes. No surprise there. She'd whacked a shin on a chair leg and bumped into the dresser while stumbling around in the inky blackness last night.

Still squinting, she lowered her arm. That's when she discovered that dazzling sunlight didn't necessarily equate to warmth. The elegant bedroom was as cold as the inside of an Eskimo's toolshed. Each breath brought icy air slicing into her lungs. It came out a second later on a cloud of steamy vapor.

Gasping, Devon dragged the covers up to her nose. Obviously, the hotel's power was still out. She knew zero about substations and transformers and such, but suspected the city that had gone dark right before her eyes last night was probably still powerless.

So where did that leave her? More to the point, where did it leave her client? Until she had a fix on the situation, she wouldn't know how to handle it.

She huddled under the covers, trying to work up the nerve to make a dash for the bathroom. The mere thought of planting her bare feet on the icy bathroom tiles kept her burrowed in.

"Devon?"

Her startled gaze flew to the door. "Yes?"

"You decent?"

"I… Uh…" She scrunched down until only her eyes showed above the fluffy comforter. "Yes."

The door opened and a man she almost didn't recognize entered the room. The cashmere overcoat and hand-tailored suit were gone. So was the boardroom executive.

This Cal Logan looked more like a cross-country Nordic skier. He wore a cream-colored turtleneck and bright blue ski jacket with the collar turned up.

Matching ski pants emphasized his muscular thighs. The pants were tucked into microfiber boots cuffed by thick thermal socks Devon would have killed for at that moment.

Luckily, she didn't have to resort to murder. Cal carried a shopping bag across the room and dumped it on her bed.

"Good thing the hotel caters to the winter sports crowd. I had the manager open the ski shop. I figured we'd both need some cold-weather gear if the power stays off for more than a day or two."

"A day or two?" Gulping, Devon tugged the covers down a few inches. "Surely they'll restore it before that."

"Maybe, maybe not. The manager said at least two-thirds of the city and most of the surrounding countryside have been affected. And it's still happening. Lines are coming down right and left."

Her gaze went to the uncurtained windows. The suite was on the sixth floor, too high up to afford more than a glimpse of the ice-coated trees lining the Elbe. From what Devon could see of them, however, most had bent almost to the ground under the unrelenting weight of the ice.

"I had to guess at your size." Cal's blue eyes skimmed down the covers and back up again. "If anything doesn't fit, I'll take it down and exchange it."

"Thanks. Er, I don't suppose you were able to scrounge some hot coffee along with the ski clothes."

"Sorry. The hotel kitchen is temporarily out of operation. The staff was scrambling to put together a cold breakfast for the guests, though." He headed for the door. "We'll go down as soon as you're dressed."

Devon dove into the shopping bag and extracted a thick pair of socks. Only after her toes were encased in thermal warmth did she grab the bag handles and make a run for the bathroom.

The toilet seat almost gave her freezer burn. The icy stream that gushed from the water taps made washing her hands and face a challenge of epic proportions. Thankfully the hotel's amenities included spare toothbrushes and a complimentary tube of toothpaste. Shivering and hopping from foot to foot, she brushed away the overnight fuzz, then shimmied into black-silk long johns so thin and sheer she wondered how the heck they could retain any heat. Her bikini briefs showed clearly through the almost-transparent silk. So did her demi-bra.

A V-necked sweater in pale lavender went on over the thermal silk undershirt. The ski pants and jacket were a darker shade of amethyst trimmed with silver racing stripes. Cal, bless him, had thought to include gloves and a headband in the same rich purple.

Ears, fingers and toes all warm and toasty, she zipped on a pair of microfiber boots and left the bathroom with a last glance at the woman in the mirror. She could use some lip gloss and a hairbrush. Hopefully, the hotel's computer whizzes would figure out some way to operate the door locks so she could get back into her own room soon. If not, she'd have to conduct another raid on the downstairs shops.

After she got some coffee in her. Preferably hot, although she'd take an injection of caffeine however she could get it right now. And food. Any kind of food. With her body's basic need for warmth satisfied, her stomach was starting to send out distress signals.

Cal stood by the sitting-room windows, taking in the frozen cityscape across the Elbe. Devon's breath caught as she went to stand beside him. Buildings, trees, the statues on the bridge, the river itself…everything as far as the eye could see lay under a blanket of glistening white. Not a single car or bus or snowplow moved through the frozen stillness, although a few brave pedestrians were making their careful way across the bridge into the Old City.

"The manager didn't exaggerate," Devon murmured, awestruck. "Looks like most of the city must be shut down."

"Looks like." He didn't sound particularly concerned as he turned and skimmed a glance over her new uniform. "How does everything fit?"

"The boots are a little loose, but you did good otherwise. Very good, actually."

The comment was more of a question than an endorsement. Logan responded with one of his quicksilver grins.

"That's what comes of having four younger sisters. We'll exchange the boots downstairs."

"We don't need to exchange them. I'll fill the space with another pair of socks."

"You sure?"

"I'm sure."

"You'd better bring your purse with you," he advised. "With the electronic locks on the fritz, we can get out but the keys won't get us back in. We'll have to leave the door propped open."

There went her lip gloss and hairbrush.

"What about your laptop and briefcase?" she asked. "Are you just going to leave them?"

"I took them downstairs earlier. They're secured behind the desk."

"We might need them to work your revised schedule if I can't get to mine."

"I think we'd better shelve any idea of work until we know the extent of the storm."

"But—"

"No buts. I'm declaring today an official holiday. All set?"

Since she didn't appear to have much choice in the matter, Devon stuffed the little evening bag she'd taken to dinner last night inside a jacket pocket and pressed the Velcro flap closed. This, she predicted silently as she and Cal descended six flights of cold, dank stairs, was going to be a looooong day.

Long, she amended some ten hours later, and inexplicably, incredibly magical.

Looking back, she saw that she and Cal had shed

their respective roles with their business suits. No longer travel consultant and client, they became co-conspirators in a determined effort to beat the cold.

Their first act was to down a surprisingly lavish breakfast. With a fervent murmur of thanks, Devon accepted a mug of the hot cocoa the hotel staff had brewed over a can of Sterno. The rich, frothy chocolate paved the way for a cold buffet of cheeses, fruits, yogurt, smoked salmon and thick slabs of Black Forest ham. Smoked over pine and coated with beef blood to give it a distinctive black exterior, the moist ham tasted like heaven slapped between two slices of pumpernickel cut from a wheel-size loaf.

After breakfast Cal insisted they don knitted ski masks and get some exercise. Devon had her doubts when the ice crusting the snow broke under her weight and she sank to her ankles. To her relief, the water-resistant microfiber boots kept her feet dry. What's more, the depressions provided just the traction she and Cal needed to join the other hardy souls who'd ventured out into the winter wonderland.

They'd gone only a few yards when what sounded like a rifle shot split the air. Instinctively, Devon hunched her shoulders and grabbed Cal's arm. He stopped her before she could drag them both facedown in the snow.

"It's just a tree cracking under the ice. Look, there it goes."

She followed his pointing finger to one of the graceful lindens lining the Elbe's banks. It was bent almost double, its branches sweeping the frozen earth. As Devon watched, the trunk groaned and split right down the middle. One half crashed to the ground. The other stood mutilated, a wounded sentinel silhouetted against the blue sky.

"Oh, how sad."

"Even sadder when you think how many other trees have split like that and brought down power lines." Cal shook his head. "Crews will have to clear tons of debris before they can repair the lines."

Keeping her arm tucked in his, he steered clear of any trees that might crack and come down on them. They made it as far as the bridge and were thinking of turning back when a lone snowplow cleared a path across the ancient stone spans.

Cal and Devon followed in its wake, as did dozens of others. They were drawn by the unmistakable tang of burning charcoal and the yeasty, tantalizing scent of fresh-baked stollen.

They followed their twitching noses to Dresden's oldest bakery. Only a block off the main square, Der Kavalier had already drawn a crowd of resilient natives and tourists determined to make the best of the situation.

Munching on the sweet, spicy bread baked in a wood-fired brick oven, they wandered down the Long Walk. The columned promenade had been erected in the sixteenth century to connect Dresden's castle with the building that had once housed the royal stables. The history buff in Devon felt compelled to point out the incredibly detailed, hundred-yard-long frieze depicting a progression of Saxon kings and nobles.

"Those are Meissen tiles. All twenty-four thousand of them. The originals were fired in the porcelain factory just a few kilometers from Dresden. Most of them had to be replaced after World War Two."

Cal dutifully admired the frieze and pumped her for more information on the city's colorful history. He did it so skillfully that Devon ran out of narration before he ran out of patience.

By then it was well past noon. They stumbled on a tiny restaurant tucked away on a side street with a kitchen powered by a loud, thumping generator. It took a thirty-minute wait but they finally feasted on steaming bowls of potato soup and black bread. Stuffed, they strolled back across the bridge only to find a wide swath of frozen river fronting their hotel had been cleared to provide space for an impromptu winter carnival.

Vendors roasted chestnuts and sizzling shish kebabs over charcoal braziers. A one-legged man muffled to the ears in scarves and a lopsided top hat cranked a hand organ. Skaters glided arm in arm to his wheezy beat. Several enterprising youngsters had overturned a wooden box and offered to rent their family's skates for the princely sum of two euros.

Over Devon's laughing protests, Cal plunked down the requisite fee. He wedged his feet into a pair of hockey skates at least one size too small and selected a pair of scuffed figure skates for Devon. When he went down on one knee to tie the laces, she made a last attempt at sanity.

"I haven't been skating since I was a kid."

"Me, either." Pushing to his feet, he dusted the snow off his knees. "Ready?"

"As ready as I'll ever be," she muttered.

He gave her a few moments to test her wobbly ankles. The next thing Devon knew, strong, steady hands gripped her waist and propelled her across the ice.

One of those hands was nestled at the small of her back when they finally returned to the hotel a little after five-thirty.

The kitchen staff had pooled its collective ingenuity to prepare another remarkable meal for the guests. Mostly cold meats and salads, with a few hot selections cooked over cans of Sterno. Spicy goulash filled the air with the tang of paprika, while bubbling cheese fondue hinted at the dry white wine and kirsch that had gone into it. For dessert, the guests were offered a choice of prefrozen Black Forest Cake and Bananas Foster flamed at the tableside.

Devon's taste buds were still sighing in ecstasy over the combination of rum and cinnamon in the flambéed bananas when she and Cal went upstairs.

They'd already been advised the electronic key-card system was still inoperable. Maintenance offered to force the lock on Devon's door, but Cal suggested she give the system another couple of hours to come online. Meanwhile, she could warm her toes in front of the fire in his suite.

When they entered the King's Suite, the rooms were as dark and as cold as a witch's tomb, yet Devon felt as though she'd come home. She couldn't believe how much she'd enjoyed her day in the bracing fresh air. Almost as much as she hated for it to end.

She could have blamed that bone-deep reluctance for what happened next. Or the hot, spiced wine she'd guzzled after skating. Or the alcohol spiking the cheese fondue and Bananas Foster.

She didn't resort to any of those excuses, however. All she had to do was look into Cal's eyes to know the day they'd just spent was merely a prelude for the night to come.

Five

After a day filled with dazzling sunlight, the night brought darkness, isolation and a swift escalation of the sexual tension that had been building between Devon and her client since their first meeting.

An intense awareness of his every move nipped at her nerves as he adjusted the gas fire. Housekeeping had been in sometime during the day and set it to burn low and steady. Cal soon had the flames leaping higher, shedding some light but little warmth beyond a radius of a few feet.

He solved that problem by dragging the heavy sofa closer to the fireplace. While he angled the sofa to catch the maximum heat, Devon lit the candles the hotel had provided its guests, along with extra blankets and a complimentary bottle of schnapps.

The schnapps she left on the sideboard but the extra blankets and two plump pillows came with her when she joined Cal on the sofa. Draping one of the blankets around her shoulders, she eyed a cordless phone nesting in its cradle on a nearby table.

"Do you think the house phones still work? I really should call my office and let them know what's happening. Or rather, not happening."

Her cell phone was in the purse stuffed in the pocket of her ski jacket. Unfortunately, she hadn't charged it before leaving for dinner last night and the freezing temperatures today had drained what little was left of the battery. Cal's mobile phone had taken a similar cold-weather hit. Between the weak signals and the saturated airways caused by so many land-lines going down, he hadn't been able to place any calls, either.

"You can give it a try," he replied, "but the cradle charger requires electricity. I'm guessing it's dead, too."

He guessed right.

They might have been alone in the universe. No TV blaring the latest financial news. No music to disturb the stillness. No phones or laptops to connect them with the rest of the world. Just the two of them. Together. With hours of quiet isolation ahead.

"This is so weird," Devon muttered, hiking the blanket up around her ears. "I never realized how much we depend on electricity. Heat, light, cooked

food, hot water, every form of communication…
They're all gone or severely restricted."

"Makes you appreciate the things we take for
granted every day," Cal agreed.

Kicking off his boots, he stretched his stocking
feet to the fire. Devon admired his seemingly philo-
sophical acceptance of the situation even as she
worried about its impact on his business. And hers.

"You told Herr Hauptmann you need to finalize
arrangements with your bankers in Berlin before
you fly back to the States on Friday. That's three
days from now. What if we're still stranded here in
Dresden, without any way to communicate with
the banks?"

"With this much money on the line, the banks will
be more than happy to work with me."

"So you were bluffing to force his hand?"

"I was taking a calculated risk. As you heard at the
meeting yesterday, Templeton Systems also made
Hauptmann an offer, but they haven't locked in the
financing yet. I want this deal signed, sealed and delivered before they do."

She blew out a silent whistle. She'd left that meeting
convinced the banks had Logan's back to the wall.

"Remind me not to get into any high-stakes poker
games with you."

His rich chuckle carried across the crackle and spit
of the gas-fed flames. "And here I was thinking a
little five-card stud might be one way to pass the
time tonight. Guess we'll have to resort to Plan B."

"Which is?"

"We talk politics. We try to guess each other's favorite movies. We wrap up in these blankets and share our body heat. We have wild, uninhibited sex."

Her jaw dropped.

"We don't have to follow that precise order," he informed her solemnly. "We could start with the sex and work our way backward."

The sheer audacity of it took her breath away. Then she saw the laughter glinting in his blue eyes, and her lungs squeezed again. Despite the wicked glint, she knew he wasn't kidding.

More to the point, she knew darn well she wanted what he was offering. Devon didn't even try to deny it. The mere thought of stretching out beside him, of feeling his body press hers into the cushions, had her heart ping-ponging against her ribs.

"What do you think, McShay?" He reached across the back of the sofa. Burrowing under the blanket draped over her shoulders, he curled a palm around her nape. "Are you up for Plan B?"

She swiped her tongue over suddenly dry lips. Her fast-disintegrating common sense shrieked at her to end this dalliance, right here, right now.

Because that's all it was. All it could be. She'd fallen for a stud like Cal Logan once and still had the scars to show for it. No way she was going to set herself up for another tumble.

So don't.

The blunt admonition came compliments of her

alter ego. The one with shivers rippling down her spine from the slow stroke of his thumb on her nape.

Have some fun, dummy. Enjoy a mind-blowing orgasm or two. Then you and Logan can go your separate ways, no harm, no foul.

Since every hormone in Devon's body was screaming at her to agree, she wet her lips again.

"I, uh, think we should start with a modified Plan B."

His thumb stilled. The gaze that had been locked on her mouth lifted to hers.

"I'm listening."

"We conduct the experiment you suggested last night. See what happens. Take it a step at a time from there."

A slow grin spread across his face. Devon's alter ego was whooping with joy even before he agreed to her proposed modification.

"Sounds good to me."

His hand tightened on her nape and tugged her closer. In the flickering light of the fire, his face was like a painting by one of the old Flemish masters, all strong planes and intriguing shadows. Then Devon's lids drifted shut, his mouth came down on hers and all thoughts of old masters, Flemish or otherwise, flew out of her head.

This kiss was slower than yesterday's. More deliberate. Despite that—or maybe because of it—the sensual movement of his lips over hers packed even more of a wallop. Devon angled her head to give him better access before surrendering to the urge she'd been battling since her first glimpse of the man shirtless.

Tugging down the zipper on his ski jacket, she flattened her palms against the broad expanse of his chest. She could feel his pecs under his turtleneck, and the jackhammer beat of his heart.

Or was that her heart pounding like a rock drummer on steroids? At this point, Devon wasn't sure and didn't particularly care. All she knew was that her other self almost wept when Cal broke the contact and lifted his head.

To her profound relief, his breath came as hard and fast as hers. The hand at the back of her neck held her steady. His eyes burned into hers.

"Well? What's the verdict? Do we progress to the next step?"

"Yes!"

She flung her arms around his neck, shedding the blanket draped over her shoulders along with any and all remaining doubts.

Cal made a sound halfway between a growl and a grunt of fierce satisfaction. His free hand tunneled under her hips. With one quick maneuver, he had her flat on her back.

His mouth was harder now, more demanding, but Devon's hunger matched his. She locked her arms around his neck and strained against him. Hip to hip, mouth to mouth, they explored the feel, the taste, the texture of each other.

He didn't ask for permission to progress to step

three. Probably because Devon was already there. Fighting free of her ski jacket, she relieved him of his, then yanked up the hem of his turtleneck and silky thermal shirt. Her hands were hot and greedy as she planed them over his back and waist and the hard, taut curve of his butt.

He wasted no time in following suit. Her lavender sweater and black silk long-john top came up and over her head with a couple of swift tugs. Her boots hit the floor next. With a speed that left her breathless, Cal peeled off her ski pants and long-john bottoms.

His hot, hungry gaze roamed from her breasts to her belly. The flesh mounded so enticingly by her black lace demi-bra brought an appreciative growl, but the matching thong stopped him cold.

"Were you wearing that thong under your dress when we went to dinner with the Hauptmanns?"

"Yes."

"And you slept it in last night?"

"Since I couldn't get back in my room, I didn't have anything else to sleep in."

"Good thing I didn't know that," he said, his voice rough, "or you wouldn't have made it out of bed this morning."

That drew a husky laugh from Devon. She wasn't any more immune to flattery than the next girl, and the expression in Cal's eyes as they devoured her nearly naked flesh was *extremely* gratifying. It almost made up for the goose bumps popping out all over her skin.

Her ensuing shiver could have been caused by the

cold air. Or the liquid fire that spread through her when he got rid of his own ski pants and long johns. Or the erection that pushed against the front of his shorts.

Her groan of dismay, however, was most definitely due to the latter. Cal's startled look prompted another groan from her, this one of embarrassment.

"I didn't mean… It's not you… Well, it is but…" As flustered now as she was aroused, she blurted out the problem. "Oh, hell! I don't have a condom. I hope you do."

"No, I don't." His lips twisted in a rueful grin. "I don't usually pack a supply for short business trips."

Unlike her ex, Devon couldn't help remembering. Blake had never left home without an emergency stash.

"I could make a quick trip down to the lobby," Cal commented. "Or…"

"Or what?"

The wicked glint returned. "We could improvise."

Devon's pulse stuttered and skipped. Oooh, boy! She was asking for trouble if the mere thought of taking him in her mouth could turn her on and her common sense off.

"You want to improvise first?" Her voice husky, she rose up on her knees and pressed her palm against his rock-hard erection. "Or shall I?"

His breath hissed out. That was all the answer she needed.

"Me," she murmured, sliding her hand inside his shorts. "I'll go first."

With a small grunt, he reached for the blanket,

whipped it around them both and followed her back down onto the sofa cushions.

They were cocooned in darkness and a heat fueled by desire. Devon used her hands and teeth and tongue, licking him, teasing him, driving him almost to the brink.

His salty taste was on her lips when she felt his body go taut. The engorged shaft in her hand seemed to pulse and swell even more. She bent her head, intending to finish what she'd started. Cal stopped her by the simple expedient of pulling free of her hold.

"Not yet," he rasped. "Not until I have my turn."

With the blanket still tented around them, he rolled her onto her back and inched downward. Slowly. As Devon had moments ago—or was it hours?—he used his hand and teeth and tongue on her eager flesh. Her nipples ached when he finished with them. Her belly quivered under his nipping kisses.

Then he spread her legs and found her hot, wet center. Once again he moved slowly. So slowly. His tongue rasped her sensitive flesh. His fingers worked sensual magic. Soon waves of exquisite sensation streaked through every part of Devon's body.

She could feel the climax coming. She tried to delay it, fought to contain the spiraling tension. She might as well have tried to contain the snow and sleet that had stranded them. Despite her determined efforts, her vaginal muscles coiled tight, then tighter still. Her head went back. A groan ripped from far back in her throat. Giving up the fight, she rode the burst of blinding pleasure.

For the second day in a row, Devon woke to dazzling sunlight. Only this time she wasn't lying in a bed topped by a majestic crown. Nor was she swathed like a mummy in a warm, insulating duvet. This time the warmth emanated from the very large, very heavy body squashing her against sofa cushions.

She lay on her side, she discovered when her sleepy haze cleared. Her back was tucked against Cal's front, with her knees bent and her bottom cradled on his thighs. Sometime during the night they'd both dragged on their thermal silk long johns. After her second earth-shattering orgasm, Devon thought lazily. As memories of the night just past came rushing back, her mouth curved into a smile. The little huff that escaped her lips was part sigh, part mewl of remembered pleasure.

As soft as it was, the sound produced a rumble in the solid wall of chest pressed against her back.

"'Bout time you woke up, Cinderella."

The blanket covering them rustled. Calloused fingertips brushed the tangled hair from Devon's cheek. Prickly whiskers rasped against her cheek as Cal scrunched around to nibble on her earlobe.

"Or was it that Snow White chick who slept for a thousand years?" he muttered between bites.

Laughing, she hunched a shoulder against the invasion of his hot, damp breath in her ear. "Someone with nine nieces and nephews should know that was Princess Aurora, aka Sleeping Beauty. And it was a hundred years, not a thousand."

"Yeah, well, Disney lost me after I had to watch a talking teapot and candlestick do their thing a half-dozen times one long, agonizing weekend."

With a final nibble, he disengaged and departed the sofa. A blast of cold air hit Devon's fanny before he tucked the blanket around her again. Only then did it register that the hotel's electricity must still be out.

"I waited for you to wake up before mounting a scouting expedition," Cal said. "Stay here and keep warm. I'll go downstairs and see if I can scrounge up some hot coffee or chocolate."

She rolled over and watched while he gathered his ski jacket, pants and boots. His cream-colored silk long johns fit him like a second skin, which made the watching a delight. As Devon's gaze roamed his broad, tapered back and trim backside, her delight ripened to a feeling of intense, almost physical, pleasure.

The front view was even more arousing. The cool, in-command executive looked more like a rough-and-tumble hockey player. His short black hair stood up in spikes. The whiskers that had rasped Devon's skin showed dark against his cheeks and chin. The spandex ski pants molded his muscular thighs, while the half-zipped jacket showed the strong column of his throat.

"Don't move," he ordered, dropping a kiss on the tip of her nose. "I'll be right back."

She fully intended to follow his instructions and remain huddled under the blanket until he returned. Unfortunately, the bathroom beckoned with increasing urgency. Dreading the prospect of another session on the icy toilet seat, Devon held off as long as she could. Nature finally conquered the cold. Shivering, she shoved her feet into her boots and dragged on her ski jacket, then sprinted for the bathroom.

When she went to wash her hands and face, the woman looking back at her from mirror gave a small shriek. Her hair was a bird's nest of dark, tangled red. Her face was devoid of all color. Except, she noted ruefully, for the whisker burn on the side of her chin. She leaned forward and fingered the tiny abrasion, then dismissed it with a shrug.

What the heck. It was small enough price to pay for the mind-bending pleasure Cal had given her last night.

See, her alter ego smirked. *What did I tell you? Is the man hung, or what?*

"No arguments there," Devon muttered.

And if the electricity doesn't come back on, you and El Stud can spend another night or two between the sheets before you go your separate ways, no harm, no foul.

"No harm," she echoed, frowning at the face in the mirror, "no foul." Somehow that didn't sound as bracing as it had last night.

Oh, come on! Don't get all hung up here. One night does not a commitment make. For you or for him.

Okay, okay! She wasn't going all gooey over the guy. Well, maybe a little, but not enough to do anything too stupid. Like fall in love with him.

She almost had herself convinced when the bathroom lights blinked on. A half second or so later, the plasma TV in the other room came to life.

"Hallelujah!"

Whooping, Devon happy-danced through the bedroom and into the sitting room. She had no idea how long it would take for the heat to kick in, but relief had to come soon. And hot water! She could shower. She could wash and blow-dry her hair. She could—

The jangle of the house phone interrupted her joyous list making. Thinking it was Cal calling from the lobby, she snatched up the receiver.

"Hello?"

A surprised huff was her only response. Maybe it was a repairman, testing the lines without expecting an answer. Someone who didn't speak English. Swiftly, Devon switched to German.

"Hallo? Ist jemand da?"

"I'm sorry. They must have put me through to the wrong suite." The voice was female, the accent decidedly American. "I'm trying to reach Cal Logan."

"This is Mr. Logan's suite."

That produced a sharp silence, followed by an even sharper query. "Who is this?"

Uh-oh. Obviously the caller hadn't expected another woman to answer Cal's phone. Then again, Devon hadn't expected to be here at this early hour of the morning answering it. Scrambling to recover, she infused her reply with crisp professionalism.

"This is Devon McShay. I'm Mr. Logan's travel consultant."

"Is that what they're calling it these days?"

The sneering comment had Devon gritting her teeth. "May I ask whom I'm speaking to?"

"Alexis St. Germaine." The reply was as glacial as the ice coating the trees outside. "Mr. Logan's fiancée."

Six

Cal balanced a cardboard tray in one hand and inserted a new key card into his suite's door lock. With the hotel's electricity restored, the computer that controlled the locks was back in operation.

Cal had mixed emotions about the return to full power. He could certainly use a hot shower and a shave, but he wouldn't have minded being left in the dark with Devon McShay for another night or two or three.

Just thinking about how he'd left her, wrapped in that blanket with her hair a tangled cloud of red and her brown eyes sleepy, got him rock hard. Which explained why he'd raided the sundries section of the lobby gift shop for condoms. With or without electricity, his plans for Devon included several more sessions under the blankets.

"The hunter returns," he announced to the woman standing beside the sofa, her arms folded across the front of her ski jacket. "We have coffee. We have fresh, crusty rolls. We have butter and strawberry jam."

She didn't leap on the hot coffee. That was his first clue something was wrong.

"We also have electricity," he said, commenting on the obvious.

"So I noticed," she said stiffly. "I'll go downstairs, retrieve a key for my room and get out of your hair."

When she started for the door, Cal deposited the tray on a side table and stopped her. "Whoa! What's going on here, Devon?"

"Nothing."

The look she flashed him said exactly the opposite. Baffled, he couldn't figure out what had caused her transformation from sleepy and sexy to ice maiden.

"Something was definitely going on last night." He tried to coax a smile out of her. "I was kind of hoping for more improvising this morning."

"I'm sure you were."

The swift retort shot up his brows. She saw his reaction and offered a strained apology.

"I'm sorry. That was uncalled for. What happened last night was as much my fault as yours."

"Fault?"

Well, Christ! Talk about being slow on the uptake.

He was dealing with a major case of morning-after regrets here.

"It was a crazy situation." She refused to meet his eyes. "The cold… The dark…"

"Funny," Cal said, attempting to smooth away the regrets, "I remember more heat than cold."

Instead of the smile he'd hoped for, all he got was a lift of her chin and a barbed reply.

"We had some fun while the lights were out, Mr. Logan. Let's leave it at that. Now it's back to business for both of us."

"The hell you say." He was starting to get pissed. "When you know me better, Devon, you'll discover I don't turn it on and off that easily."

"Don't you?" Disdain and something very close to disgust darkened her eyes. "Oh, before I forget, your fiancée called a few minutes ago. She heard about the ice storm on the news. She's been worried about you and wants you to call her back as soon as possible."

"That's interesting," Cal said, his eyes narrowing, "since I don't happen to have a fiancée."

"You'd better inform her of that. Now if you'll excuse me, Mr. Logan, I'll leave you to make your calls and go make mine." Her chin came up another notch. "Assuming you still want EBS to work your travel arrangements, that is."

The realization that she thought he was the kind of slime who would sleep with one woman while engaged to another pissed Cal even more.

"Yes, *Ms*. McShay, I do."

"Fine. I'll work the revised itinerary and get back with you."

This wasn't over between them, Cal vowed as she made for the door. Not by a long shot. He'd make that clear shortly. First, he had to deal with Alexis.

His temper simmering, he had the phone in hand almost before the door snapped shut behind Devon. He punched in the country code for the U.S., followed by the number of the Park Avenue apartment he'd leased for Alexis St. Germaine some months ago.

"It's Cal," he bit out when she answered.

"Darling! I've been so worried about you. The news has been running the most awful stories of derailed trains and fifty-car pileups all across Europe."

The husky contralto brought back instant memories of the first time Cal had heard it. He'd been dragged to one of his sisters' charity soirees. It was a crowded, noisy affair, but Alexis St. Germaine had turned the head of every male in the room.

Cal had walked off with the prize, although even then he'd suspected the stunning blonde was more interested in his bank balance than in him. After a particularly energetic tussle, he'd teased her about it. Alexis had laughed and admitted she had extravagantly expensive tastes and always made it a point to marry well. She'd also admitted she'd lined Cal up in her sights as husband number three the moment he'd walked into the charity ball.

For several months, he'd almost convinced

himself they might make a go of it. Alexis was smart, sophisticated and the center of attention at every party. Only gradually did Cal realize his fiancée craved an audience like a junkie craved a fix. After an endless round of cocktail hours, dinners at expensive watering holes and pre- and post-theater gatherings, he'd called it quits.

He'd insisted she keep the four-carat solitaire and arranged to transfer the Park Avenue apartment into her name, but Alexis wanted more. She hadn't come right out and threatened a breach-of-promise suit, but just last week her lawyer had dropped a hint that Cal might want to consider a reconciliation.

"I called your office," she told him. "When they said they hadn't heard from you, I envisioned you in the hospital or trapped in train wreckage somewhere."

"I'm fine."

"I know. Now. Your, ah, travel planner assured me you'd both survived the storm."

The casual comment contained a question Cal had no intention of answering.

"I miss you, darling. When are you coming home?"

"What do you want, Alexis?"

He knew damned well there was more to her call than concern for a stranded ex-fiancé. Sure enough, her husky laugh came over the line.

"You know me so well. We really should try again. Why don't we get together for the holidays?"

"I don't think so. You'll be partying, and I've got a deal to close."

"What company are you trying to buy now?"

"One you've never heard of."

"Well, don't spend all your billions on it, darling. I went a little crazy at Bergdorf's the last few weeks we were together. The bill arrived in the mail yesterday."

So that was it. Cal's mouth curved in a sardonic grin.

"Send it to my office. I'll take care of it."

"I knew you would," she purred.

"Consider this a Christmas present, Alexis. And just so we're clear, this is the last 'gift' from me until you nail husband number three. That will certainly merit a wedding present."

The unsubtle warning produced another rippling laugh.

"Don't count yourself out of the running yet."

"Idiot!"

Devon stalked across the lobby, still kicking herself for the conversation in Cal's suite.

She'd handled it all wrong. She'd intended to play it cool, not brittle and bitchy. So he was engaged? Or not, depending on who she listened to. So he cheated on the woman who still obviously loved him? That was his problem. His, and Alexis St. Germaine's.

There was no reason Devon should feel like The Other Woman. But she did, dammit. She did!

As she skirted the giant Christmas tree by the front desk, all she could think of was that awful evening she'd walked into her husband's office and found him getting hot and heavy with a giggling

Santa. Only this time, she was the getter and Cal was the gettee.

God! How stupid could one person be!

"Devon McShay," she told the desk clerk. "I need a new key for my room."

"Right away, Ms. McShay." The young woman was muffled to her ears in a heavy coat and wool scarf and obviously relieved to have the power back on. "It's good, yes? To have the lights and the computers again?"

"It is."

"And the tree," she added, nodding to the giant fir dripping handcrafted ornaments and silver garlands. "What is Christmas without colored lights?"

Devon returned an inarticulate response and pocketed the key. She'd hoped this trip would keep her less-than-joyful memories of the holiday season at bay. Instead, she'd have a whole new set to add to the grab bag.

"Idiot," she muttered again.

The hotel's heating system was starting to chase away the chill when she let herself into her rooms. Her junior executive suite was a fourth the size of Cal's palatial arrangement. Yet after the tumult of the past two days and nights, Devon reveled in the privacy and having access to her own things.

Shrugging out of the lavender ski jacket, she made a beeline for the bathroom. Her number-one priority was a shower. Cautiously, she tested the water. It was gloriously, deliriously hot.

"Thank God!"

Stripping, she adjusted the oversize showerhead to full force and stepped into the glass cubicle. The stinging jets needled into her skin. She stood with her face upturned for long moments, letting the punishing stream pour over her, before lathering up and washing away the sticky residue of the night spent in Cal's arms.

Scrubbed, shampooed and near scalded, she wrapped a towel around her head and one of the hotel's plush terry-cloth robes around her tingling body. The superfast heating coil Europeans used to boil water produced an almost instantaneous mug of coffee. Sipping the life-restoring brew, Devon padded to the desk and flipped up her laptop.

Number-two priority was reworking Cal Logan's itinerary. The sooner she got him to Berlin and Hamburg and on that flight back to the States, the sooner she could put this whole sorry episode behind her.

The screen came to life, and the e-mail icon that popped up indicated forty-three incoming messages. At least half were from her partners, she saw as she scrolled through them. Sabrina and Caroline had both become increasingly worried about how Devon was faring through the storm and blackouts affecting most of Western Europe.

She zinged off responses that her partners wouldn't read for some hours yet. It was still the middle of the night back in the States. Sabrina and

Caroline were both sawing z's. Unlike Ms. St. Germaine, who'd stayed up until the wee hours trying to reach Cal.

Fingers flying, Devon searched the Internet for status reports on the travel situation in and around Germany. Her pulse leaped when she saw the high-speed trains between Dresden and Berlin were once again up and running.

The train station was only a few blocks away. If the streets had been plowed and sanded, they could get a taxi and catch the eleven-fifteen express. A quick call to the front desk assured her a few hardy taxi drivers had braved the weather and were parked outside. She booked the last two first-class seats on the express and was about to call the Berlin hotel to make sure they still had rooms when a sharp rap on her door interrupted her feverish activities.

Devon squinted through the peephole and bit back a curse. She wasn't prepared for Cal yet. Not with her hair wrapped in a towel turban and the rest of her naked under the terry-cloth robe. For a cowardly moment, she was tempted to ignore his knock.

Oh, hell! She had to face the man sooner or later. Might as well get it over with. Summoning a cool, businesslike smile, she unhooked the chain and opened the door.

"Good timing. I was just about to call you with an update."

She could hardly brief him in the hall, but the mere thought of inviting him inside ratcheted up her stress level. He'd showered and changed, too. His black hair gleamed with dampness. Above the open collar of the blue dress shirt she'd purchased in the gift shop, his face was clean-shaven. Recalling the red mark left by his raspy whiskers, Devon clutched the collar of her robe with one hand and gestured him inside with the other.

"I've booked us on the eleven-fifteen express train for Berlin. I'll confirm our hotel reservations for tonight and we'll be good to go."

"Not quite. We need to clear the air first."

"You're right. We do." Dragging in a deep breath, Devon took the lead. "I apologize. Again. I had no right to get all huffy with you earlier. We're both adults. Last night was…"

Incredible. Mind-boggling. The wildest sex she'd ever experienced.

"…fun," she finished, wincing inside at the total ridiculousness of the adjective. "You may not believe this after our, uh, activities, but I'm not usually into one-night stands."

Her stiff little speech stirred his temper. She could see it in his eyes, hear it in his drawled retort.

"You may not believe this, but I'm not, either."

She scrubbed the heel of her hand across her forehead. He wasn't exactly making this easy, dammit.

"Look, whatever arrangement you have with Ms. St. Germaine is between you and her. I'd just rather not be part of it. I had enough of that sort of thing with my ex."

Hell! She hadn't meant to let that out. Her brief marriage and its sordid demise were no one's business but hers.

She could see her slip had registered with Cal, though. His expression lost a little of its hard edge as he hooked his thumbs in the pockets of his pants.

"First, Alexis St. Germaine and I are not engaged. We were, but we called it off before I left on this trip."

"The woman must be delusional, then. She seems to think you're still a twosome."

"She's not delusional, but she is extravagant. I paid the bills she ran up when we *were* a twosome. She just got a few more in she needed help with."

Devon bit her lip. Evidently Cal hadn't scored any better in his choice of a mate than she had.

"Second," he continued, his gaze drilling into her, "the last word I'd use to describe our activities last night is 'fun.'"

That brought her chin up. "Really? Then how would you describe them, Mr. Logan?"

"How about the start of something that could lead us down any number of paths, *Ms.* McShay?"

She rubbed her forehead again and tried to sort through her jumbled emotions. Her lascivious alter ego was jumping for joy over the fact that Cal was not, in fact, engaged. Her other, more rational self was every bit as relieved but far more cautious.

"About last night being the start of something," she said finally. "I'm not sure this is the right time for either of us. You've just ended a relationship."

More or less. Ms. St. Germaine obviously still needed convincing.

"And my partners and I are just getting our new business off the ground," she said doggedly. "With you, I might add, as our first major client."

"I don't see a problem."

"Then you're a lot better at compartmentalizing than I am," she retorted. "I'm having some trouble shifting back and forth between Cal Logan the client and Cal Logan the stud."

"That last bit is a compliment, right?"

His hopeful look drew a huff of reluctant laughter from Devon. "Mostly."

"Good. You had me worried there for a moment."

He was doing it again, she realized. Using humor to bypass her doubts and undermine her resolve. Her laughter fading, Devon pressed her point.

"The very fact that you weren't sure if it was a compliment only emphasizes how little we know each other."

"What do you want to know?" He leaned his hips against the back of the sofa and crossed his arms. "Ask me anything. Age. Weight. Shoe size. Whether I prefer sausage or pepperoni on my pizza."

"I'm serious, Cal."

"So am I. Ask away."

"Much as I would like to take you up on your offer, I have to remind you we're booked on the eleven-fifteen express to Berlin. I still need to confirm our hotel rooms and get packed. And," she added, her mind clicking on the tasks ahead, "I need to take the gifts you bought for your nieces and nephews down to the business office for packing and FedExing. And see what's happening with your lost luggage. And call for a taxi. And get us checked out."

And blow-dry her hair.

And put on some makeup.

And scramble into some clothes.

With a small rush of panic, Devon had a sudden mental image of the silver bullet express pulling out of the station while she ran after it, screaming at the damned thing to wait.

"Okay," Cal conceded. "We'll table this discussion for the time being."

She heaved a sigh of relief as he shoved away from the sofa.

"You work the phones and pack," he instructed, shifting into executive-decision mode. "I'll take the kids' stuff down to the business office, get us checked out of the hotel and have the front desk call a taxi."

He shot back his cuff, checked his watch and whistled. "Can you be ready in a half hour?"

Like she had a choice? "I can."

He crossed to the door and yanked it open, then paused.

"By the way, the correct answers are thirty-one, one-eighty, size ten and pepperoni." His grin came out, quick and slashing. "And just for the record, I don't consider getting to know you better and getting you into bed again to be mutually exclusive."

Seven

They made it to the train station with exactly twenty minutes to spare.

Miracle of miracles, Cal's leather carryall and suit bag had been delivered and were waiting at the front desk when he went down to check out. He'd managed a quick change into a fresh suit, a crisp white shirt and a red tie for the three-hour trip to Berlin. Devon had scrambled into her stacked-heel boots, gray wool slacks, an off-white turtleneck and her heavy winter coat. The hot pink pashmina fluttered behind her like a cape as she and Cal jumped out of the cab and hit the crowded station.

Stranded travelers thronged the ticket booths, all anxious to get to their chosen destinations for Christmas after the horrendous delays caused by the storm. Since Devon had booked their tickets online and printed them at the hotel's business center, she and Cal didn't have to fight the crowds at the booths. There was another logjam at the gate, but they got through it just as the two-minute departure warning sounded.

The high-speed bullet train hummed on its track, as eager as a thoroughbred at the starting gate. Cal slung his suit bag over his shoulder and shifted his carryall and briefcase to one hand so he could relieve Devon of her roller bag while she made a dash for the first-class coaches. With his longer legs, he kept up with her easily.

Mere seconds after they jumped aboard, a final warning sounded and the doors glided shut. Devon led the way to their reserved seats and flopped down, breathless.

"We made it!"

"So we did," Cal said as the train started to move.

He stashed their bags in the overhead compartment and swiveled his airline-style seat around to face hers. They had a small table between them and, when the train pulled out of the station, a bird's-eye view of Dresden's Old City through the wide windows.

The spires and turrets rose above the frozen River Elbe, a sparkling, ice-coated panorama Devon knew she would never forget. She propped her chin on her hands and drank in the view until apartment buildings obscured it. Sighing, she swung around to face Cal.

"Quite a city," he commented, shrugging out of his overcoat. "If this deal with Hauptmann Metal Works goes through, I'll have to make several return trips." The skin at the corners of his eyes crinkled. "Think you can work it so we don't get buried under ice next time?"

Devon didn't know which pronoun carried more interesting implications. The "you" that indicated he wanted EBS to handle his future trips to Germany or the "we" that suggested she would be traveling with him.

"I'll do my best to skirt the ice," she replied. "You didn't have a message from Hauptmann waiting on your cell phone?"

"No, but I didn't expect one. If it were me, I'd wait until the last minute and try to work some extra concessions in terms of salary adjustments and stock options."

He helped Devon out of her coat and hung it alongside his on the hooks attached to their seats. The train was picking up speed now and zipping through the city's outskirts. The urban sprawl soon fell away, giving passengers glimpses of the fascinating blend of culture and history that had prompted UNESCO to declare this strip of the Elbe river valley a World Heritage Site.

Elegant eighteenth- and nineteenth-century suburban villas with terraced gardens and elaborate facades perched atop the riverbanks. Ironwork bridges from the dawn of the Industrial Revolution spanned the frozen Elbe at several crossings. Small towns and villages dotted the landscape. From the distance, the stucco and half-timbered farmhouses appeared much as they must have in previous centuries.

"Hungry?"

The question drew her gaze from the rolling countryside. They'd missed breakfast in the rush, or at least Devon had. Cal may have feasted on the crusty rolls and strawberry jam he'd brought up to the suite before she'd marched out in a huff.

"I'm starving," she admitted, "but they won't start serving lunch in the club car until noon."

"That's only twenty minutes from now. Hang tight. I'll scrounge a couple of menus. We can check 'em over while we wait."

He headed for the door to the next car, moving with an easy grace that accommodated for the swaying motion of the train. Devon wasn't the only one who followed his progress. Several people looked up as he passed. The men's glances soon returned to their newspapers. The women's tended to linger several seconds longer.

With good reason, Devon admitted ruefully. His suit had obviously been tailored by a master. The red silk tie had probably cost more than her entire outfit. It wasn't just the clothes that snagged those lingering glances, however. It was the way he wore them, the way he carried himself. That air of unmistakable self-confidence and power turned most women on, big time. Devon included.

Hey, she told her sniggering other self. *I'm only human.*

The problem now was what to do about the contradictory emotions Cal Logan roused in her. In the flurry of frantic, last-minute activities, she hadn't had time to process what he'd told her about his fiancée. Make that ex-fiancée.

Nor had she let herself think about the zinger he'd tossed out just before he'd left her hotel room. That bit about getting to know her and getting her into bed again not being mutually exclusive now jumped to front and center in her mind. It was still there when Cal returned with the menus, two cups of hot chocolate and two slices of stollen.

"First seating in the club car is all booked up. I reserved a table for the second seating. I figured this would tide us over until then."

They attacked the sticky-sweet Christmas bread and hot chocolate with equal fervor. Devon was savoring her last bite when Cal stretched out his legs and regarded her across the littered table.

"So tell me about this jerk you were married to."

She threw him a startled glance. "Did I say he was a jerk?"

"I extrapolated. So tell me."

Sighing, she fiddled with her fork. "There's not much to tell. We met, we married, we discovered we had different interpretations of monogamy. I thought it meant one mate for life. Blake thought it meant one wife but lots of mating on the side."

She stabbed at the crumbs on her plate. Even now, she kicked herself for not picking up on the signs sooner.

"How long were you married?"

"Less than a year." Her mouth twisted. "We got engaged on Christmas Eve and flew to Vegas for a quick wedding three weeks later. The following Christmas Eve I walked into the television station where he works and found him, uh, exchanging gifts with the station manager."

"Male or female?"

"Female," she said with a small laugh. "Thank goodness! My ego took a bad-enough bruising as it was."

As soon as the words were out, Devon realized their truth. She'd been hurt and furiously angry, but looking back she could see her pride had been dinged as much as her heart.

"Is that when you decided to go into business with Sabrina Russo?"

"No, I hung around Dallas for a few years. The idea of starting EBS didn't come up until Sabrina and Caroline—our other partner—and I got together for our annual reunion last spring. The three of us were roommates in college," she explained. "Only for one year. At the University of Salzburg, as part of a study abroad program."

"Salzburg, huh? That must have been an incredible experience."

"It was!"

Devon jumped on the change of subject.

"The whole time we kept thinking we'd landed smack in the middle of a remake of *The Sound of Music*. When we walked to classes each morning, we went past the convent featured in the movie. I swear to goodness, you could hear the nuns chanting on their way to Mass."

Smiling, she shared her memories of that year in the fairy-tale Austrian city.

"I was a history major, so I dragged my poor roommates to every castle and museum in or around the city. Caroline's an opera buff. She made sure we didn't miss a performance at the Salzburg Opera House. Sabrina, on the other hand, got us personally acquainted with most of the city's *Biergartens* and *Ratskellers.*"

Cal chuckled. "Brown Eyes, also known as the good-time girl. That's how my pal, Don Howard, described her. Guess the shoe fits."

"It did then," Devon admitted, bristling a little in defense of her friend. "Sabrina's changed. All three of us have. That's why we decided to start EBS. We needed to refocus our lives and couldn't think of a better way to do it than by combining our resources and the experience we gained while living abroad."

"I hope the combination works for you."

"Why wouldn't it?"

"You said your dad's an accountant. I'm sure he's told you that in any partnership, someone always ends up having to make the tough financial decisions. I'll bet he's seen a lot of friendships sacrificed to the bottom line. I certainly have."

"You won't see these."

"I'll take your word for it," he said easily. "Now to the important stuff. What do you like on your pizza?"

* * *

By the time the train pulled into Berlin's new glass-and-steel megastation, Devon knew she was dangerously close to falling for Cal Logan, and falling hard.

He was so damned easy to be with. He'd entertained her for a good part of the journey with stories about his various sisters and brothers-in-law and their numerous progeny. She'd reciprocated by telling him a little more about her parents and their still-stormy relationship years after the divorce. Yet even as she and Cal lingered over dessert and coffee in the luxuriously appointed club car, swapping family histories, the physical hunger the man roused in her increased with every shared laugh, every seemingly casual touch.

There was nothing the least casual about the protective arm he put around her shoulders as they wove through the jostling crowds inside the station, however. Or the possessive hand he nestled against the small of her back to steer her toward the rank of taxis. She'd intended to call from the train and order a limo, but Cal nixed the idea since their hotel was only a few blocks from the station.

As soon as the cab pulled away from the terminal, the hustle and bustle of Germany's vibrant capital enveloped them. Devon knew from news reports that the ice storm hadn't hit Berlin as hard as it had Dresden. She saw the truth of that in the traffic and pedestrians clogging the sanded streets and sidewalks.

Unlike Dresden, which had been restored to its earlier glory after the devastation of World War Two and the bleak years of Communist domination, a new city had risen from the ruins of Berlin. The ultramodern skyscrapers of Pottsdamer Platz dominated the skyline. The Sony Center's towering, circus-tent–like dome of glass and steel sparkled in the bright afternoon sun. Windows in the pricey shops and department stores lining Friedrichstrasse showcased designer boots and bags and clothing—all displayed against backdrops of silver snowflakes or green-and-red Christmas paraphernalia, of course.

Devon tried not to let the crass commercialism dampen her pleasure at returning to a city brimming with history and world class museums. And even she caught her breath at the hundreds of live poinsettias lining the magnificent staircase leading up to the lobby of their hotel. More poinsettias were tiered to form a thirty-foot-high Christmas tree in the center of the lobby.

"We'll have to hustle," Cal warned after they'd checked in and hit the elevators.

He'd called ahead to set up a late afternoon meeting with his contacts in Berlin. That barely left them time to dump their bags and freshen up.

"I'll meet you in the lobby in fifteen minutes," Devon promised.

Her room was on the eighth floor, his suite on the tenth. When the elevator door pinged open, she grabbed her roller bag and started to exit. Cal held the door with a bent arm, but blocked her way. A crooked grin tugged at his mouth as he resumed his stated campaign to get her into bed again.

"Sure you don't want to share a room? We did pretty well the last two nights."

Oh, yeah, she wanted to share! After those hours on the train, with the easy conversation and comfortable camaraderie, Devon had advanced *her* stated goal of getting to know Cal better. So much better, the mere thought of kissing that smiling mouth and exploring the hard, muscled body under the hand-tailored suit made her throat go dry.

"We're down to fourteen minutes and counting," she said a little breathlessly. "How about we make that decision when we get back?"

Cal's grin when he dropped his arm and stepped back into the elevator told her the decision was already made.

The grin stayed with Devon as she hurried down the hall to her room. Once inside, she flung her suitcase onto a luggage rack and dropped her brief-case onto the desk before dashing to the bathroom. Hair combed, face scrubbed and makeup reapplied, she had time for one quick call and a voice mail for her partners on her way out.

"In Berlin. Off to a meeting with Logan. More later."

Much more later, she thought as she hurried back down the hall. The question of just how much had her pulse pounding and anticipation singing along her veins.

* * *

The taxi delivered Devon and Cal to the Daimler-Chrysler Center, a mini-city of towering high-rises interconnected by walkways, parks, shops and restaurants. Although it was barely four-thirty in the afternoon, the tall buildings crowded out the sun and threw deep shadows across the plaza. To counter the early evening gloom, white lights blinked everywhere—in leafless tree branches, in shop windows, in restaurants. Her arm tucked in Cal's, Devon hurried through the tunnel of lights toward the skyscraper housing the German headquarters of Bancq Internationale.

As he had at the meeting with Herr Hauptmann, Cal included her in the session with the financial advisors. Devon might as well have remained in the outer offices while the half-dozen men and three razor-sharp women hammered out the details of the proposed acquisition. They threw out so many numbers and terms like minority equity stakes and venture capital line of credit she was soon lost.

The meeting lasted for several hours. It was a working session, with suit jackets discarded, ties loosened and sleeves rolled up. Although Devon was more of an observer than a participant, she felt as whipped as the other men and women at the table when Cal finally called a halt.

"We've got the basic structuring down. I'll e-mail these figures to my people so they can go over them tonight. We'll make any necessary adjustments when we get together again tomorrow afternoon. By then," he added as he unrolled his sleeves and shrugged into his suit coat, "I should have heard one way or another from Herr Hauptmann."

Since they hadn't been sure when they would arrive in Berlin, Cal had already declined an offer of dinner and an evening on the town with the firm's senior executives. That, too, was rescheduled for tomorrow.

"Leaving us free tonight," he murmured provocatively to Devon as the elevators whisked them down to the plaza.

Like she needed reminding!

The sudden spike in her pulse erased the mind-numbing effects of three-plus hours of financial analyses. She could feel her heart thumping against her ribs when she and Cal emerged into a night that had come alive with big-city vibrancy.

Diners were jammed elbow-to-elbow in the pubs and restaurants, while last-minute Christmas shoppers packed the pricey boutiques. Carolers in Victorian-era costumes occupied a raised platform in center plaza. Their voices amplified by speakers, they sang of shepherds keeping watch over their flocks and wise men traversing great distances.

For the first time in more Christmases than she could remember, Devon found herself actually enjoying the carolers and the crowds. Much of that, she admitted silently, had to do with the man at her side.

Okay, all of it. The eagerness she'd felt as a young child, before her parents' acrimonious fights had turned the holidays into a war zone, didn't come *close* to the anticipation now zinging through her veins.

She had no idea where this…this association with Cal Logan might lead. As he'd said, it could take them down any number of paths. Or it could end in Hamburg, when they boarded their separate flights back to the States.

But that wouldn't happen until Friday morning. They still had two full days, and two nights, together. She was reminding herself of that fact when Cal stopped and sniffed the air.

"I smell tomatoes and garlic and…"

"Pepperoni," she finished, laughing. "Why do I have the impression pizza is your favorite food group?"

"Maybe because it is. I pretty much lived on junk food when I was a teenager. After I joined the Marines, I'd slop up my SOS and try like hell to convince myself it was hot, crusty pizza."

"What's SOS?"

"You don't want to know." He tugged on her arm. "Come with me, woman. I think it's only fair I wine and dine you before I have my way with you."

She had to protest, if only for form's sake. "I thought we deferred that decision."

"You deferred, I decided."

That sent Devon's simmering anticipation to a near boil. She felt its heat as they made for the lively, crowded Italian restaurant across the plaza. They were shown to a table after only a short wait. By then their imminent return to the hotel so dominated her thoughts she was amazed she could get down a single slice, never mind the three Cal insisted on heaping onto her plate.

He was just as generous with the wine. It was a rich, full-bodied Dornfelder that more than held its own against the spicy pizza sauce. Although by no means a wine connoisseur, Devon had spent enough time in Germany to know the hybrid red Dornfelder grape was grown mostly in the Rheinhessen and Pfalz regions, but was gaining in popularity throughout the country.

With good reason, she decided when she and Cal returned to their hotel. The buzz was mild on its own, but potent as hell when combined with the heat that roared through her the minute the elevator door swished shut and Cal backed her against the rear wall.

Eight

"People get arrested for this sort of thing," Devon panted.

"Only if they get caught."

Her back was to the mirrored elevator wall. Her mouth was greedy under Cal's. Her breath coming in eager gasps, she popped the buttons on his overcoat and burrowed under the layers.

She'd tried to put the brakes on. Tried to rein in her hunger for this man. Now the walls had come down and she didn't even think about holding back. The taste of him, the feel and the scent him, torched every one of her senses.

She didn't feel the elevator slow, but Cal did, thank God. He disengaged a half second before the doors slid open. Devon had a good idea what she must look like, though, with her lip gloss smeared, her cheeks flushed and her hair tumbling free of its clip. Still, she managed a smile and a nod for the elderly couple that stepped into the elevator.

"Guten abend."

The silver-haired woman returned the greeting. Her husband glanced from Cal to Devon and back again. Cal returned his knowing smile with a bland one of his own, yet his unbuttoned coat and lopsided tie told its own tale.

A moment later the elevator glided to a stop on Devon's floor. Mere moments after that, the door to her room slammed shut and she and Cal were tearing at each other's clothes.

Mouths hot, hands impatient, they left a trail of outer garments from the door to the bed. Cal kept an arm banded around Devon's waist as he yanked down the duvet, then took her with him to the satiny-smooth cotton sheets.

The first time they'd made love had been in the cold and dark. Huddled under a tented blanket, Devon had explored with her hands and mouth and tongue. This time she intended to feast on the sight of the powerful body pressing her into the mattress.

Attacking his shirt buttons, she dragged it free of his pants. Her palms felt the heat as she moved them over his chest, his shoulders. The tight, bunched muscles set her heart hammering against her ribs. She could almost feel the endorphins shooting into her bloodstream as the muscles low in her belly clenched.

With an impatience that matched Devon's, Cal stripped off the rest of his clothes and went to work on hers. Her boots hit the floor with a thud. Her wool slacks and turtleneck followed a moment later.

"Well, damn!"

The low exclamation brought Devon up on one elbow. "What's the matter? Oh, no!" Groaning, she answered her own question. "Please don't tell me we're condomless again."

"No, I laid in a good supply."

"Then what...?"

"I didn't think anything could turn me on more than that black thong and bra you were wearing the other night." His grin came out, quick and delighted. "I was wrong."

Shifting her under him, he slid a palm inside the waistband of her lacy hipsters. Her stomach hollowed under his touch, and every nerve in her body snapped to attention when he slowly tugged them down. Her bra went next. Then he was all over her, teasing, tormenting.

He used his tongue and teeth to bring her nipples to tight, aching peaks. The heel of his hand cupped her mound. His thumb pressed her hot flesh, and his fingers...his fingers worked sheer magic!

Eager to give as good as she got, Devon wrapped her hand around the erection poking at her hip. It filled her palm, hot flesh over hard steel, and made her crazy to feel it fill the rest of her.

"Now," she panted. "Now is a good time to find that supply you mentioned."

Grinning, Cal thrust off the bed and snagged his slacks. Devon was wet and ready and impatient as hell as he ripped open a condom. When he repositioned himself between her thighs, she hooked her legs around his calves and took him into her body.

It wasn't until the next morning that she realized she'd also taken him into her heart.

Sometime during the night, Cal had kicked down the last of her protective barriers. Maybe during their second supercharged session, when she'd straddled his hips and ridden him to an orgasm that ranked right up at the top of her all-time-great list. Or just before dawn, when he'd nudged her awake and made slow, lazy love to her.

Whenever it had happened, Devon felt happily, ridiculously content as Cal leaned over her and dropped a kiss on her cheek.

"I'm going up to my room to shower and change."

"Mmmm."

"You sleep in for a while. I'll take your key and bring you breakfast in bed."

Devon snuggled for a little while longer before realizing she couldn't lie there and wait for him all sticky and fuzzy from sleep. She dragged to the bathroom, turned on the shower and leaned against the glass stall. Eyes closed, she let the jets pelt life into her boneless body. With the tingling came memories of the night just past and a silly, goofy grin.

Watch it, kiddo. You were just supposed to have some fun.

She'd definitely had that!

Remember what happened the last time you fell for a charmer like Logan.

This was different. *Cal* was different.

You met him all of…what? Three days ago? How do you know he's different?

She knew. She wasn't sure how she knew, but she knew. Or so she told herself as she cut off the pesky thoughts along with the shower jets.

She emerged from the bathroom sometime later dressed and ready to face the day. Her first order of business was to update her partners. It was well past one in the morning back in the States, so Devon flipped up the lid of her laptop, intending to type out a detailed e-mail. To her surprise, she saw that Sabrina and Caroline were online and conducting a video chat. Quickly, she keyed in her password and joined the session.

"Hi, guys. Why are you both up so late?"

"We're talking business."

Sabrina's face filled one half of the laptop's screen. Her long blond hair was pulled back in a scrunchie, and her eyes were bright. Not with fever, Devon was relieved to learn, but with excitement.

"We got a new contract this afternoon," Sabrina

related. "A big one, but it's another quick turnaround. Caroline and I have been working the prelims."

"Who's the client?"

"Global Security, International. From what we've uncovered so far, the company started out as a band of mercenaries hired to provide personal protection for top Iraqi government officials. It's since evolved into one of the largest—and most lethal—security agencies in operation around the globe."

Devon was as anxious as her partners for their fledgling company to succeed, but she wasn't particularly thrilled at the idea of donning a helmet and flak vest.

"They don't want us to work their travel and provide escort service in and out of Iraq, do they?"

"No, thank goodness. We've been tasked to scout out locations and finalize arrangements for an off-site gathering of their key personnel in late January or early February."

"They specified Italy or Spain," Caroline put in. "Something close to the ocean. We're thinking the Amalfi Coast south of Naples as one possibility, Barcelona or the Costa Brava as the other."

Devon thought fast. She was supposed to fly back to the States on Friday, the same day Cal departed. She could change her reservations and travel by way of Naples or Barcelona or both.

The click of the door lock distracted her momentarily. She glanced over her shoulder, waved to Cal and turned back to the screen.

"Do you want me stay over in Europe?" she asked

her partners. "I could fly from Germany to Italy, scout out possible locations for this conference and hit Spain on the way home."

"Oh, Dev." Caroline's forest green eyes filled with sympathy. "I know how this time of year scratches at old scars, but you don't want to spend Christmas shuttling between countries. Come home and spend it with us."

"Sorry." The deep voice came from just over Devon's left shoulder. "As it turns out, I'm going to require EBS's services longer than originally anticipated. If Devon agrees, she'll be spending Christmas with me."

Startled expressions crossed the two faces on the split screen.

"That's Cal," Devon explained.

She could feel her cheeks heating and was fumbling for an explanation for his presence in her bedroom this early in the morning when he bent down. The camera in her laptop's lid merged his face with hers.

"Hello, ladies."

Caroline merely nodded in response to this unexpected intrusion into their business, but Sabrina gave a low, gurgling laugh.

"So you're Don's buddy. Thanks for delivering the long overdue—if completely misdirected—kiss."

"It was my pleasure."

His warm breath stirred the hairs at Devon's temple and sent little shivers rippling down her spine.

"I'd better go," she told her partners. "I'll send

you an e-mail with this potential change in our client's schedule."

Signing off, she slewed around in her chair. "As soon as said client tells me what it is," she added pointedly.

He leaned forward and planted his hands on the arms of her chair. Caged, she looked up into blue eyes blazing with the satisfaction of a hunter who's just bagged his prey.

"I had a message from Herr Hauptmann when I checked my calls a little while ago. He's agreed to my terms for the buyout."

"Cal! That's great! Congratulations."

He tugged her out of the chair for a celebratory kiss. Devon gave it joyously. After sitting in on the meetings in Dresden and here in Berlin, she almost felt part of the Logan Aerospace team herself.

"Hauptmann wants to set up another meeting to sign the necessary paperwork and work the final details of the merger. We agreed on the first week in January. I thought I'd bring my key staff over then to tour the plant and confer with their counterparts."

"So you want EBS to work your travel arrangements?"

"I want EBS to work my *staff's* travel arrangements. I've decided to stay in Europe over the holidays. I'm hoping you'll stay with me."

"But… But… You said you always spend Christmas with your family. All those nieces and nephews. What happened to playing Santa?"

His mouth curved. "You happened."

Her heart stuttered, stopped and started again with a painful thump.

"I've been to almost every major city in Europe," he added, tucking a stray curl behind her ear, "except Salzburg. After listening to you describe it yesterday, I thought we might spend Christmas there."

Beautiful, magical Salzburg. In midwinter, when it was dressed in snowy white. With Cal Logan. Devon melted into a puddle of want on the spot.

Cal's smile widened as he read the answer in her face. "We could fly down to Austria after the meeting in Hamburg tomorrow. Think you can work the travel arrangements and a hotel room on short notice?"

She noted his suggestion of a single room even as her head whirled with yet another change in plans. All they had on the schedule today was a second meeting with the finance people this afternoon and dinner with the firm's senior execs tonight. She had until then to work the arrangements.

"You go play with your numbers." Waving a hand, she shooed him away. "I'll hit the computer."

Devon zinged off a quick e-mail to her partners detailing the latest developments. The rest of the morning she was on her laptop, arranging the trip to Salzburg and laying the initial groundwork for a meeting between Cal's key staff and that of Hauptmann Iron Works.

The mood was jubilant when she and Cal met

with his financial wizards that afternoon, and the thrill of victory imbued the air during dinner at one of Berlin's finest restaurants.

The same high spilled over to a more private and *much* more erotic celebration when Devon and Cal returned to the hotel. Seemingly inexhaustible, he took her to the edge of the precipice three or four times before intense, unstoppable pleasure finally drove her over.

They left Berlin early the next morning for Hamburg, Germany's second-largest city. It was only a few hours away by high-speed train. Called the Venice of the North, the city was situated on the wide mouth of the Elbe. The river that meandered across Germany and provided such a scenic setting in Dresden provided Hamburg with direct access to the North Sea. As a result, it had been a rich sea-trading center and leading member of the Hanseatic League as early as the Middle Ages.

Cal's sole purpose for the visit was to tour the massive Airbus production facility located on the banks of the Elbe. Logan Aerospace had several contracts for navigational aids used in the aircraft. In addition, Cal wanted to see firsthand the extent of Hauptmann Metal Works contracts. Devon had arranged for a limo to meet them at the train station and deliver them directly to the Airbus plant.

The tour ran longer than expected. During lunch in the executive dining room, the plant manager offered Cal the opportunity to meet with the engineers responsible for integrating all navigational aids. That might have presented a problem if Cal hadn't canceled his plans to fly back to the States that afternoon as originally scheduled. Luckily, Devon had reserved seats on an early evening flight to Salzburg.

She wasn't too thrilled at the idea of another four or five hours at the Airbus production facility, however. The discussion had veered into technospeak well beyond her comprehension and had deadened her initial awe.

Cal must have noticed the way her eyes glazed over at the prospect of spending the rest of the day listening to him talk product specifications and redesign. When they finished lunch, he asked for the use of an office to make some calls. Devon used the time to make a few of her own. Their respective business taken care of, he offered her an escape.

"You don't need to hang around here all afternoon. Why don't you take the limo and go downtown? Since you'll be staying in Europe several weeks longer than planned, I'm sure you need to pick up a few things."

More than a few! She could use hotel laundry and dry-cleaning services for the outfits she'd brought with her, but two pants suits, four tops, one long skirt and the skiwear Cal had purchased in Dresden weren't going to hack it for an extended stay.

She almost salivated at the thought of hitting Hamburg's famous Mönckeberg Strasse. The Mö, as the natives liked to call their favorite shopping street, rivaled New York's Fifth Avenue and Beverly Hills' Rodeo Drive for high-end boutiques and ultra-elegant department stores.

She'd been a backpacking student traveling on a Eurorail Pass and a limited budget during her only other visit to Hamburg. She still couldn't afford to shop the designer boutiques, but she *could* do some serious damage in the department stores.

She was happily making a mental list when Cal reached into his suit pocket for his wallet and extracted several bills.

"This should cover what you need. If not, just give me a call and I'll authorize a line of credit."

As Devon stared at the bills, her little bubble of anticipation fizzled and went as flat as two-day-old champagne. Only yesterday he'd told her about picking up the tab for his extravagant former fiancée. Now he was offering to do the same for her.

"That's…" She swiped her tongue over suddenly dry lips. "That's very generous, but I don't need you to pay for my personal necessities." She lifted her gaze to his. "Or anything else."

He looked at her blankly for a moment. Then his brows snapped together. "Christ, Devon. I hope to hell you're not implying what I think you are."

When she didn't answer, his eyes went cold.

"I've asked you to extend your stay in Europe to handle the meeting between my staff and that of Hauptmann Metal Works. Naturally, Logan Aerospace will cover your expenses."

Confronted with his obvious anger, she tendered an apology. "I'm sorry if I jumped to the wrong conclusion, but…"

"*If?*"

The acid comment stiffened her spine. "I told you I'm not as good at compartmentalizing as you are. I'm still trying to separate the client from the…"

"Stud," he finished, his jaw tight.

He didn't appear to find the label as amusing as he had yesterday. Neither did Devon.

"I'll spell it out for you." He dropped the bills in her lap. "Logan Aerospace will cover any expenses you incur incidental to the business portion of this trip. Make sure you get receipts. My accountants will expect an itemized listing when EBS submits its final bill."

Nine

Dammit all to hell!

Cal administered a swift mental kick as he accompanied his escort down the mile-long corridors of the Airbus production facility.

He'd handled that scene with Devon wrong. He shouldn't have lost his cool or acted like such a stiff-necked jerk. After what he'd told her about Alexis, no wonder she'd jumped to the wrong conclusion.

Still, the fact that she *had* mistaken his motives put a severe dent in his pride. It also pissed him off. Royally. Did she really think he'd intended to buy her? Or that he would be stupid enough to mix his personal finances with that of his business?

The dig hit at something deeper, though. Something he hadn't stopped to analyze until this moment. He'd wanted Devon McShay from their first meeting, when he'd tugged her into his arms and delivered Don's kiss to the wrong woman. Cal hadn't exaggerated when he'd told her about the kick to the gut he'd experienced there at the Dresden airport. If anything, he'd understated the issue.

In the days since, his hunger for her seemed to have taken on a life of its own. Every touch, every stroke of his hands over her warm, smooth flesh, fed the beast in his belly. He got hard just remembering her taste, her scent, the feel of her slender body under his.

Yet the craving wasn't simply physical. Sometime in the past few days it had gone beyond mere attraction. He knew now he wanted more from Devon than the admittedly intense pleasure she gave him.

The problem was, he couldn't decide what that "more" constituted. Just weeks ago he'd ended an engagement to a woman he'd felt the same kind of hunger for…at first. Alexis was nothing if not stunningly seductive. And to her credit, she'd made no secret of the fact she considered Cal's wealth and power among his chief attractions.

By contrast, Devon went to almost the opposite extreme. The woman was as stubborn as an Arkansas mule when it came to the business side of their relationship. So stubborn, she couldn't—or wouldn't—separate the client from the man.

Correction. Stud.

Cal's simmering irritation took a sardonic turn. Okay, he had as much ego as the next guy. He'd made a joke of the tag when Devon first laid it on him. Truth be told, it had put a little strut in his walk. He wasn't strutting now.

Which brought him back full circle. Why the hell was he so pissed? And what did he want from Devon?

He'd better figure that out before he met up with her again in a few hours.

What did Cal want from her?

More to the point, Devon thought as she threaded through the shoppers thronging the Mö, what did she want from *him?*

Shoulders hunched against the damp fog that rolled in from lake across the boulevard, she paid little attention to the store windows festooned with Christmas displays. Cal's wad of bills burned a hole in her coat pocket.

Her rational mind knew he was correct in insisting Logan Aerospace cover expenses incident to her extended stay in Germany. Her less rational and wholly emotional self couldn't shake the nasty thought he was paying for services unrelated to EBS.

She caught her reflection in a shop window and made a moue of disgust. She looked as miserable and confused as she felt.

"It's this time of year," she muttered under her breath to her reflection. "It always makes you crazy."

Yeah, it does. So what are you going to do about this particular crazy?

If she had an answer to that, she wouldn't be standing on the sidewalk, talking to a store window!

What she needed, she decided, was to talk to her business partners. They had the distance, the separation, to view this issue objectively. That they were also her closest friends might muddy the water a bit, although Devon didn't see how it could get any muddier.

She checked her watch and saw it was almost three o'clock here in Hamburg. That would make it close to nine in the morning back in Virginia. Caroline and Sabrina had stayed up late last night working the new contract, but, knowing her partners, she bet they were both up and at it again.

Eager to talk to them, Devon cut over a block and pushed through the revolving doors of Alsterhaus, Hamburg's most famous department store. The multistory facility was large and elegant and a favorite with locals and visitors alike. It offered all kinds of products, from stationery and fashion and fine wines to the latest electronics and CDs. The top-floor restaurant featured a superb view of Lake Alster and the canals and waterways.

Devon lucked out and got a corner table by the windows. It was private enough for a conversation with her partners but still offered an incredible view. Although she'd consumed a working lunch with Cal and the Airbus brass in their executive dining room, she couldn't resist a bowl of Hamburg's famous eel soup.

She'd sampled it on her previous visit and knew the soup base was a clear broth flavored to a sweet-and-sour edge by vinegar and sugar. Finely sliced carrots, leeks, dried plums, pears, apples and small dumplings simmered with the broth. The eel, sliced a half-inch thick, weren't added until the last minute. Devon wasn't real big on eels, but the ones fished from the northern reaches of the Elbe tasted more like chewy chicken than fish.

She chose a dry white Rheingau to sip while waiting for her soup, then hit the speed-dial number for the office. Both Sabrina and Caroline were already at work. Wishing she had her laptop so she could see their faces, Devon responded to Caro's demand to know where the heck she was now.

"Still in Hamburg. Cal's meeting with Airbus is running later than anticipated."

Sabrina chimed in, her voice filled with her ready laughter. "Good thing we decided on flexibility as one of our primary operating parameters. Will you have to rework your connections to Salzburg?"

"Yes. No. Maybe."

"What does that mean?"

"It means I don't know if I'm going to Salzburg."

"Why not? I thought it was all set."

"I thought so, too." Sighing, Devon stared unseeing at the glass-topped tour boats plying the gray waters of Lake Alster. "That was before Cal opened his wallet and handed me a stack of bills to buy whatever I needed for our little play date in the Alps."

Stark silence greeted her statement. Sabrina was the first to break it. "Surely he wasn't that crass."

"No. He couched the gesture as a cost of doing business. He thinks Logan Aerospace should cover any expenses I rack up as a result of staying over to work the conference of his key personnel."

"Okay, now I'm officially confused. What are we talking here? The conference or your play date in Salzburg, as you so delicately term it?"

"*You're* confused!"

Out of deference to the other diners in the busy restaurant, Devon managed to refrain from wailing into the phone. Barely.

"Everything's happened so fast. I feel as though I've been riding a nonstop bullet express since the moment I met Cal Logan."

"Can't you slow the express down?" Caroline asked, her voice warm with concern.

"I've tried! Believe me, I've tried. I told Cal I wasn't any good at mixing business and pleasure. I insisted we should get to know each other better before jumping into the sack again."

"That didn't work?"

"It did and it didn't. We talked for hours on the train between Dresden and Berlin." She let out a long sigh. "Then we hopped right back into bed."

"Is he that hot?" Sabrina wanted to know.

"And then some," Devon said on a half laugh, half

groan. "He's also funny and thoughtful and smart and very take charge."

"Uh-oh."

"Exactly! Every time I think I have a handle on where things are going between us, he'll say or do something that throws me completely offtrack. Like this business with the cash. Do you think I over-reacted to his offer to pay my expenses?"

"No!" Caroline said with swift, fierce loyalty. She, too, carried the scars left by the one man she'd let herself love. Hers went deeper than Devon's, though, and at her express wish were never discussed.

"Yes!" Sabrina countered just as swiftly. "You're staying over in Europe at Cal Logan's request to set up a conference. Logan Aerospace should cover any business-related costs."

"Which doesn't include a holiday tryst with the CEO," Devon pointed out.

"It's your call, Dev," Sabrina said, her voice softening. "Don't go to Salzburg *or* work the conference if either one will cause you grief."

"I second that," Caro said staunchly. "With the contract we just landed, EBS doesn't need Logan Aerospace."

All three women knew that was a gross exaggeration. Even with the new contract, their fledgling business was a long way from recovering the initial start-up costs and turning a profit.

"Sabrina and I trust your judgment explicitly. Do what your heart and your head tell you is right."

* * *

Devon's head and heart debated the issue right up until it was time to go back for Cal.

In a last-minute compromise, she used her personal credit card to purchase a few necessities. They were stuffed in her roll-on when the limo pulled up at the visitor's entrance to the Airbus production facility.

She remained in the car, waiting for Cal, her gaze on the Elbe. This far north, the river was broad and flat and gray, its midchannel current too strong to freeze over as it had in Dresden. Across the river, the ruins of a watchtower and castle sat atop a strategic hill. Lining the bank below were pricey condos and small resort hotels, interspersed with boat docks and rowing clubs.

A flurry of movement at the front entrance caught her attention. Cal strode out, his cashmere overcoat slung over his arm. The wind ruffled his dark hair as he said goodbye to the Airbus execs. Watching him, Devon tried to sort through the welter of contradictory emotions the man stirred in her.

It wasn't just his physical presence, although she'd be the first to admit he gave new meaning to tall, dark and gorgeous. It was more his unique blend of sophistication and humor, of power and personality. She'd seen him in action in the boardroom, knew he could go for the jugular. Yet she'd also seen him in secondhand skates, the tip of his nose red from the cold and his eyes alight with laughter as he propelled her across the ice.

Then there was the instant heat he ignited with every touch, every kiss. Her hormones had been working overtime since that first meeting in the Dresden airport. And that was the problem, pared down to its core.

Devon had mistaken lust for love once. She wouldn't—*couldn't*—make the same mistake again.

Briefcase in hand, Cal headed for the limo. When he slid into the seat beside her, his expression showed none of the anger of a few hours ago. But his glance held a distinct challenge when it met hers.

"Did you find everything you needed?"

"That depends," she said carefully as the driver put the limo into gear.

"On?"

"On what we decide after you hear what I have to say."

She smoothed her gloved hands over the flaps of her black wool coat. She'd had plenty of time to rehearse her speech on the way back to the Airbus plant.

"Here's the deal. We've already established that I'm not as skilled as you are when it comes to separating personal and professional relationships. The misunderstanding earlier this afternoon made that painfully obvious. So I think we choose which of the two relationships we want to nourish."

"I thought I'd made *that* painfully obvious. I want you, Devon."

The answer caused a flutter just under her ribs but didn't tell her what she needed to know. With a swish of the soft leather seat, she angled around to face him.

"I want you, too. So much I can't think straight. Which is why I can spend the weekend with you in Salzburg or I can arrange your conference, but I can't do both."

"Can't, or won't?"

"Okay, won't."

He accepted that with a small nod, his gaze thoughtful as he studied her face.

"Just to clear the air," he said slowly, "I'm not trying to buy you by throwing a little business your way. Having you work the conference seemed like a win-win situation for both EBS and Logan Aerospace."

It was, Devon admitted silently, until the lines between lust and love began to blur and left her feeling her way blindfolded through a potential minefield.

"I know that's how it's done in the business world," she conceded. "It was the same in academia. You scratch my back by helping me research my article in the *Journal of Medieval History.* I'll scratch yours by reworking the outline for next semester's graduate course on the Italian Renaissance. Things have a way of getting complicated, though, when the back-scratching turns physical."

A gleam of amusement softened his eyes. "More complicated for you than for me, apparently."

"If that's your way of saying I'm being overly cautious, you're right. A botched marriage has a way of doing that to a girl. Not that we're talking marriage," she added hastily. "Or anything close to it."

Maybe *she* wasn't, but Cal had spent the past few

hours analyzing more than product specifications and redesign parameters.

The more he'd thought about his irritation at Devon's response when he'd offered to pay her expenses, the more he realized how arrogant he must have sounded. Consciously or un, he'd placed her in the same category as Alexis. As though she was someone whose career he might boost. Someone he could assist financially. Someone who needed him.

Only gradually had the hard truth sunk in. Unlike Alexis, Devon McShay was dead set on making it on her own. Her stubbornness had annoyed the hell out of him at first. Irritation had given way to grudging acceptance, then an admiration that got all mixed up with the other feelings the woman roused in him.

He wanted her with a hunger that seemed to feed on itself. The wanting grew with every hour in her company, every smile she sent his way, every stroke of his palm over the curve of her breasts or belly. Cal had walked out of the Airbus production plant determined to keep Devon in his life—and in his bed— for the foreseeable future.

Now she'd drawn a line in the sand. He could have her or her professional services, but not both.

"So who's supposed to make the decision?" he asked. "You or me?"

"I've already made it." Her gaze held his, clear and unwavering. "I'd rather spend Christmas with you than land a million in new contracts."

"Good." Grinning, Cal slid a hand under the soft

fall of her hair and hooked it around her nape. "If the answer had been any different, I wasn't letting you out of this car until I'd changed your mind."

He tugged her close for a kiss that left her breathless and him hurting like hell. Flushed and obviously relieved that he'd acquiesced so readily to her decision, she flopped back against the leather seat.

Cal didn't burst her bubble. He had acquiesced. To a point. He wouldn't push the issue right now, but during the next few days he *would* employ every one of the skills he'd acquired over the years to convince Devon she couldn't put him—or herself—into nice, neat boxes.

He came with Logan Aerospace attached. She was EBS. When they merged, so would their business interests.

During the drive to Hamburg airport, Cal began to contemplate a completely different sort of merger. The idea took shape slowly as he listened to Devon's bubbling, infectious enthusiasm over spending a few days in her all-time favorite city.

"Salzburg any time of year is wonderful, but it's absolutely magical in winter. I can't wait to show you all my favorite haunts."

"I hope that doesn't include all those museums and ruined castles you told me about."

"Only a few," she admitted, laughing. "I'll go easy on you. Thank goodness the city doesn't get as jam-packed with tourists in winter. Especially over the holidays. They're all home, doing the family thing."

She hesitated, her eagerness tinged with a touch of guilt.

"Are you sure you don't mind not playing Santa for all those nieces and nephews?"

"I'm sure. What about your folks?" he asked, searching her face. "Were they disappointed that you won't be with one of them for Christmas?"

"Not particularly." She hunched her shoulders in a mock shudder. "Each of them would have spent the entire time griping about the other, so I'd already decided to spend the holidays with Caro and Sabrina instead. They're my real family."

Something twisted inside Cal. He'd grown up surrounded by the large, boisterous Logan clan. Even in the Marines, when he'd been stationed halfway around the world and couldn't get home for the holidays, his parents and sisters had inundated him with letters and phone calls and packages crammed full of goodies he'd shared with his entire platoon.

He thought of the lonely Christmases Devon must have spent while he listened to her plans for their time together.

"I want to take you to the Opera Haus. And maybe we can get in some skiing. Caro and Sabrina and I spent every hour we could on the slopes during our year in Salzburg."

"Either one sounds good."

"Oh, Cal! You're going to fall in love with Salzburg, just as I did."

Smiling, he curled a knuckle under her chin and tipped her face to his. "I'm already there."

She looked a little startled, but before he could elaborate, the limo glided to a stop at the terminal. Devon snagged a cart for their few pieces of luggage while Cal tipped the driver.

"We'd better hustle," he said, slinging their cases onto the cart. "We don't want to miss the flight."

Ten

The joyful clanging of Salzburg's cathedral bells pulled Devon from sleep. She lay still, her backside tucked against Cal's thighs, his arm a dead weight on her waist, and savored the happiness that spread through her. She'd returned to her favorite place in the world. Birthplace of Mozart. Home to one of the world's great music festivals. Repository of her eager, youthful dreams.

She couldn't believe she was back after all these years. Or that she was sharing the magic with Cal.

Rather than stay at one of the big chains, she'd booked them into a small hotel in the historic heart of the city. The hotel nestled right up against the old Roman walls, almost in the shadow of the castle that rose high above the copper roofs and cupolas of the *Altstadt.*

They'd arrived too late yesterday evening to do more than feast on Wiener schnitzel and pan-fried potatoes at the hotel's restaurant and take a stroll through the brightly illuminated Christmas market that filled the main square.

Ah, but today, Devon thought as the bells sang to her, today she'd show him the city she'd fallen in love with so many years ago. Almost quivering with anticipation, she wiggled her butt.

"Hey, big guy! You awake?"

"I am now."

His voice was lazy and amused. The rest of him, it turned out, was anything but.

His arm tight, he drew her closer. She could feel him hardening against her rear, feel his breath warm on the back of her neck.

"I can't think of a better way to start the day," he murmured, inserting his knee between hers.

She thought about protesting for all of two or three seconds. She needed to hit the john, splash the sleep from her face, attack her teeth. Those minor considerations evaporated when Cal leaned forward and nipped the tendons in her neck. Her little shivers of delight had him fumbling for one of the condoms on the nightstand.

"We're going to run through your whole supply at this rate," Devon muttered.

"I'll restock," he promised as he slipped his arms around her waist again.

He slid in. Slowly. Stretching her. Filling her. Pulled out. Slowly. Until just the tip tormented her eager flesh.

Then in again. Out again. The pace was maddening, but the sensations incredible. They spread from Devon's belly, one piling on top of the other, making her grind her hips against his and squeeze every one of her muscles as tightly as she could.

She felt Cal go rigid behind her, heard his breath hiss out. She squeezed harder. He went over the edge with a long, low grunt. She fell off a few seconds later.

Devon lay in his arms, her body joined with his, until the world stopped spinning. "Heck of a way to start our first day in Salzburg," she got out after a minute or two.

"Heck of a way to start *any* day," he agreed, nuzzling her hair.

Her energy seeped back in slow degrees. With it came her eagerness to show Cal her favorite city. Rolling over, she dropped a loud, smacking kiss on his chin and pointed a stern finger at the bathroom.

"Okay, fella. You first. And make it quick. We have things to do and places to go."

Fortified by a hearty breakfast, they bundled up in their ski gear and sallied forth.

After the beautiful but treacherous ice of Dresden and the cold, drizzly fog of Hamburg, Salzburg offered sparkling sunshine and a blanket of clean snow. The steep peaks ringing the city wore skirts of white. More snow dusted the church steeples and copper roofs of Old Town. Designated a UNESCO World Heritage Site for its cultural and historical significance, the city was divided into two halves by the winding Salzach River. And from every street corner was a view of the magnificent Hohensalzburg Fortress high atop a hill overlooking the city.

Christmas added a special, festive air. Colored lights twinkled in every window. Garlands fashioned from fragrant pine boughs wrapped every streetlamp. The resiny tang provided a sharp counterpoint to the mouthwatering aromas of roasting chestnuts and sizzling sausages, while the scent of fresh baked bread poured from every bakery and corner café.

People thronged the streets. Skiers with their skis and poles over their shoulders brushed elbows with native Salzburgers in traditional loden green coats and alpine hats sprouting pins, feathers or brooms. A scattering of hardy tourists craned to see the sights while huddling under blankets in open, horse-drawn carriages. Shoppers jammed the main squares and multitude of Christmas markets, snatching up last-minute gifts and goodies.

Avoiding the crowds, Devon took Cal to her favorite places. The library at the university with its incredible collection of illuminated manuscripts, which she'd spent so many hours pouring through when she should have been cramming for exams. Salzburg's monumental baroque cathedral, where Mozart was baptized and later composed many of his sacred works. The tiny *Weinstubbe* tucked away on a narrow street that served the best goulash in the city.

They departed the restaurant in late afternoon with their bellies full and their palates on fire from the paprika in the goulash. Arm in arm, they descended a flight of snowy steps. Devon had intended to take him to the funicular for the ride up to the castle and its panoramic views of the city, but the small crowd gathered outside a narrow building at the base of the stairs caught Cal's attention.

"What's this?"

Devon skimmed the plaque beside the door of the modest eighteenth century house. "Joseph Mohr was born here. He wrote the poem that later became the lyrics to 'Silent Night.' His house is a museum, but it's closed now."

"So why the crowd?"

She made a polite query and got several enthusiastic responses.

"This group is taking a sleigh tour to the chapel in Oberndorf where 'Silent Night' was first performed. A local choir does a special Christmas Eve performance there each year."

"You talked about taking a sleigh ride. Why don't we go, too?"

Just in time, Devon managed not to grimace. She wasn't into organized tours at the best of times, and schmaltzy tours like this one held even less appeal. But this was Cal's first visit to Salzburg, and it *was* Christmas Eve. He'd given up being with his family for her. She could go schmaltzy and touristy for him. Still, she felt compelled to issue a word of warning.

"They say the chapel in Oberndorf is miniscule. It only accommodates fifteen or twenty people. So the performance is held outside."

He skimmed a glance over her knit cap, pink pashmina and down-filled ski gear. "Will you be warm enough?"

"I'm good if you are."

"Great. Let's see if they can squeeze us in."

Devon fully expected the tour leader to shake his head regretfully. Special tours like this were no doubt sold out months in advance. The group had four no-shows, however, and the organizer promised Devon and Cal a seat in one of the sleighs if the missing four didn't turn up in the next ten minutes.

They didn't.

Sternly quashing her doubts, Devon climbed into a minivan with Cal for transport to a farm on the outskirts of the city. There the group transferred to horse-drawn sleighs that held six passengers in addition to a driver perched on a high front bench. Supplied with flasks of hot chocolate and snuggled under warm blankets, they set off with a stomp of hooves and the merry jingle of harness bells.

The track cut through a stand of snow-draped pines, and someone two sleighs back started singing. Soon the whole group was belting out "O Tannenbaum." Devon buried her chin in the folds of her scarf to hide another grimace.

* * *

Three hours later, she knew she'd broken the Christmas curse forever. No matter where she was or what happened in the years to come, this night would always, *always,* remain in her mind and her heart.

Her breath steamed on the cold evening air as she stood hand in hand with Cal among a crowd of several hundred. They formed a semicircle in front of the tiny chapel. Spotlights illuminated the hexagonal structure with its cupola dome. Tall pines, their branches heavy with snow, formed a dramatic backdrop behind it. Above, stars gleamed in a sky turning from dark blue to black.

A local priest had said Mass in the open air, accompanied by a choir in Austrian dress singing traditional hymns. With the Mass over, the choir began the carol everyone had come to hear. The famous strains of "Silent Night" lifted to the starstudded sky.

The choir sang the first few choruses in the original German, inviting the crowd to join in. Other languages followed. Devon had no difficulty with the German and Italian versions and picked out most of the French phrases. Cal's rich baritone soared during the English chorus.

Standing there in the cold, her hand gripped in his, Devon felt the painful memories from years past fade into insignificance. One by one, her old hurts dissipated. Layer by layer, her cynicism peeled away.

This was what she'd always longed for, she

realized. Not the gifts her parents had heaped on her in their never-ending competition to buy her love. Not the endless parties and spiked eggnog.

Just this cold, starry night. This quiet joy. A man like Cal to share it with.

The last notes of the last chorus faded into the night. No one moved. The stillness was as beautiful and consuming as the singing. Finally, someone stamped their feet against the snowy earth and the crowd began to drift toward the tour buses and sleighs. Cal needed to make a pit stop, so he and Devon joined the horde heading for the gift shop/museum set well away from the chapel.

While she waited for him, it occurred to her that he'd just given her the most remarkable gift of her life, but she didn't have anything to give him in return. She scanned the trinkets and souvenirs but couldn't find anything that suited her. Hoping she'd have time to hit a shop or two in Salzburg, she met Cal at the entrance.

Once they had climbed into their sleigh, he put his arm around her shoulders and pulled her close. The driver checked to make sure his passengers were all aboard and snuggled in before flicking the reins and calling to his team. The two plow horses stomped their hooves, snorting gusts of air through their nostrils, and strained against the harnesses. Bells jingling, they fell into an easy gait.

The village of Obendorf soon faded into the night, and the track once again cut through thick stands of pine. The trip out had been filled with laughter and song. The return was quiet.

Devon leaned against Cal, wrapped in his warmth. Her chin was tucked deep in the folds of her borrowed pink scarf. His lips nuzzled her temple.

"Thank you for tonight," she said softly. "I needed it. I didn't know how much until I stood there, listening to the choir."

"You're welcome."

Devon spent the rest of the ride back to the farm reflecting on this incredible night. She climbed into the van for the trip to town, absolutely convinced it couldn't get any better.

She was proved wrong the moment she and Cal walked into the restaurant at their hotel. She stopped dead, her disbelieving gaze locked on the two people at a table close to the stone hearth.

One of the occupants spotted her at almost the same moment. With a glad cry, she tossed down her napkin and shoved back her chair.

"Devon!"

Leaping up, Sabrina rushed across the room. Caroline followed a moment later. The three friends fell into each other's arms for a noisy, laughing group hug.

"I can't believe it!" Devon exclaimed when she got her breath back. "When did you guys get here?"

"A few hours ago. We would have been here earlier, but the flight out of Frankfurt got delayed."

"But… But I thought you were flying into Rome,"

she said to Sabrina, as confused as she was delighted. "And Caro was supposed to head for Barcelona to check out sites for our new contract."

"We changed our reservations after Cal's call," Sabrina informed her.

"Cal's call?" Devon repeated stupidly.

"He wanted it to be a surprise." Her friend's sparkling glance went to the man standing a little to one side. "Looks like we pulled it off."

"Looks like we did," Cal agreed. "By the way, Brown Eyes, I have something for you. This is from Don."

Grinning, he dropped a kiss on Sabrina's cheek before turning to the third member of the group.

"And you must be Caroline."

Caro took the hand he held out. Quiet and reserved by nature, she was slower to open up to strangers than the effervescent Sabrina. Cal got one of her rare, unguarded smiles, though.

"I am."

She started to say more but was interrupted by the arrival of another group of guests.

"We'd better move out of the way." She led the way back to the table. "We waited to order dinner. You haven't eaten yet, have you?"

"No," Cal answered. "We joined a Christmas tour and took a sleigh ride out to the country. We just got back."

Two pairs of astonished eyes turned toward Devon.

"A Christmas tour?" Sabrina echoed. "You? The

original Ms. I-don't-have-time-for-all-this-holiday-hype?"

An embarrassed flush warmed Devon's cheeks. Shrugging, she returned a sheepish grin. "I'm resigning my membership in Grinchettes Anonymous."

Caro reacted to the news by reaching over to squeeze her friend's hand. Sabrina merely shifted her glance from Devon to Cal.

"Well, well." A teasing smile tugged at her lips. "So there *is* a Santa. Where's your beard?"

"I'm going for a more generic look. How are you feeling?"

"All recovered. Sorry I canceled out on you at the last minute."

"I'm not."

He leaned back in his chair and hooked an arm over the back of Devon's. The possessive gesture wasn't lost on either of the other two women. Their almost identical expressions told Devon to expect an intense grilling later.

She had another matter to clear up first. Angling around, she faced Cal. "When did you call Caro and Sabrina?"

"The day after you agreed to spend the holidays with me here in Salzburg."

"But… I thought…"

"I know. We were supposed to use this time to get to know each other." Raising a hand, he tugged on a strand of her hair. "I keep telling you, Ms. McShay. I know all I need to know."

Across the table, Sabrina and Caro exchanged two very speaking glances.

"You mentioned your friends were flying over right after the holidays," Cal continued, his smile tender. "You also mentioned the three of you are closer than sisters. So I thought this would be a good way for you to have your family with you at Christmas."

Devon's heart melted into mush right there at the table. He'd given up being with the family he obviously adored but had arranged for her to be surrounded by those she loved. Which, she realized on a hot rush of emotion, included Caleb John Logan, Jr.

What an idiot she was! She'd been so afraid to trust her heart, so worried her instincts were flawed after the fiasco of her marriage. Instead of reaching out and grabbing love with both hands, she'd tried to hold it at arm's reach while she analyzed and dissected her feelings.

No more, she vowed fiercely. No more! From now on, she'd take her chances on life *and* love.

"You couldn't have given me a more perfect gift," she said with a catch to her voice. "Thank you. Again."

"You're welcome. Again."

While she basked in the utter joy of the moment, a rueful gleam entered his eyes.

"I have to confess I had ulterior motives. I still want EBS to work the Logan Aerospace conference. I thought this would be a good way for me to meet your business partners. And," he added with a wicked grin, "for them to convince you it doesn't make sense to turn down a lucrative corporate contract just because you have a thing for the CEO."

Devon gave a sputter of helpless laughter. She knew darn well she should be pissed over this blatant end run. It was hard to work up a good mad, though, when Cal had dressed the maneuver up with such a big red bow.

"I'll discuss the matter with my partners," she conceded.

"You do that." He gave her hair another tug. "Now how about we order? I'm starving."

The restaurant offered a set menu that night featuring traditional Austrian Christmas Eve specialties, with fried carp as the main course and chocolate-and-apricot Sacher torte for desert.

The four Americans weren't the only ones who lingered over coffee and the sinfully rich torte. Visitors from other countries shared the flickering glow from the fireplace. Devon listened with half an ear to a spattering of French, Sicilian-accented Italian and what she thought was Portuguese. Her mind wasn't on the murmured conversations going on around her, though.

Her chin propped in her hands, she watched her friends and Cal interact. Sabrina, with her tumble of sun-streaked blond hair and laughing eyes, engaged him in a lively give-and-take. Even dark-haired and usually-so-serious Caro responded to his teasing with lighthearted quips.

As her gaze roamed the small circle, Devon knew

she didn't want this night to end. Ever. She understood, though, when the inn's owner came by each table to wish his patrons a blessed Christmas and remind them the restaurant would close several hours early so the staff could spend the rest of the evening with their families.

Cal must have sensed her reluctance to abandon her friends. As he retrieved her jacket from the back of her chair, he checked his watch.

"It's still early back home. Why don't I go up to the room and make a few calls while you three have some girl time?"

"Some girl time would be good," Sabrina replied, hooking her arm through Devon's before she could wiggle out of the intense grilling she knew would follow. "We'll send her up in a little while."

Nodding, Cal gave Devon a quick kiss and said good night to her friends. He'd barely disappeared around a corner before Sabrina dragged Devon to a cluster of armchairs in a corner of the lobby.

"Sit!" she commanded. "Talk! Omit no detail!"

Eleven

Devon thoroughly delighted Cal when she wedged into the small shower with him on Christmas morning and insisted on soaping him down. And up. And down again.

The sudsy activities led them right back to bed. Flushed and eager, she pushed his shoulders flat on the mattress and straddled his hips. Her auburn hair was a wild tangle of wet curls from the shower. Her skin was slick and smooth and so creamy he wanted to lick her like a cherry-vanilla triple-dip ice-cream cone. She licked him instead.

The third gift didn't arrive until breakfast. Cal and Devon were down before Sabrina and Caroline and had the small dining room to themselves. A fire already danced in the hearth. A sweet, yeasty aroma wafted from the kitchen. In honor of the occasion, the owner of the small hotel was dressed in his Sunday best. Sporting a ruffled shirt, bright red suspenders and a gray jacket with brass buttons and the green traditional facings, he bustled out of the kitchen with a carafe of coffee and a plate of braided bread bursting with raisins and currants.

"Fröliche Weinachten!"

Smiling, Devon returned the greeting. "Merry Christmas to you, too."

"My wife bakes this stollen herself for our guests. We are happy to have you with us on this blessed day."

"Thank you."

"We prepare only a light breakfast this morning, yes? Then, after church, we have the goose."

"Served crisp and still sizzling," Devon told Cal as the manager went back to the kitchen. "With dumplings, potatoes, curly kale, brown gravy and steins of dark, foaming beer."

His stomach did a happy roll in anticipation of the feast. The rest of him was as delighted when she reached for his hand and threaded her fingers through his. Her warm brown eyes were luminous in the early morning light. Her smile made him want to bundle her right back upstairs.

"In case I forget to tell you later," she said softly, "this is my best Christmas ever."

That hit Cal like a fist to the gut. He thought of the chaos that would ensue when his boisterous clan descended the stairs of his parents' Connecticut home in about eight hours. The kids would squeal and attack the mounds of presents. His sisters and brothers-in-law would try to keep some semblance of order for two or three minutes before giving it up as hopeless. His folks would revel in the noise and mess.

From the little she'd told him, Devon had never experienced that kind of exuberant celebration. She would, he vowed fiercely. Next year.

Lifting their entwined hands, Cal brushed a kiss across the back of hers. "It's one of my all-time greats, too."

He'd planned to wait, give her the time she kept insisting she needed. Trouble was, he'd never been good at marking time. If he hadn't jumped at opportunities when they came along, he wouldn't have turned a small electronics firm into a multinational corporation. And this opportunity was just too good to pass up.

"I'm thinking we should to do this on a more permanent basis."

Her startled glance met his. Cal saw confusion in her face, along with a sudden wariness that made him want to pound the bastard who'd hurt her into a bloody pulp.

"I want more holidays with you, Devon. Easter. July Fourth. Groundhog Day."

Her hand jerked in his. Reflex action, Cal thought, until her nails dug in. He saw what he was hoping for in her golden brown eyes. He couldn't have received a gift that thrilled him more.

"I want the other days, too," he warned, raising her hand for another kiss. "Lazy Sunday mornings reading the paper. Thursday evenings at our favorite restaurants. Weekends once in a while with my folks. And yours, if they can—"

"Merry Christmas, you two!"

Sabrina's cheerful greeting floated across the small dining room. She punctuated it with a waggle of her brows when she noted their joined hands.

"Uh-oh! Looks like I'm interrupting something. Want me to go away?"

Cal smothered a curse and reminded himself that he was the one who suggested Devon's friends fly to Europe a few days early. Rising, he pulled out a chair for her.

"Yes, you're interrupting," he said with a grin, "and no, we don't want you to go away. Devon and I were just talking about holidays."

Sabrina plopped down and tore off a piece of the still-warm bread.

"God, this is good!" Between bites, she picked up on Cal's comment. "And speaking of holidays, what's the plan for New Year's? I'm booked at the resort I want to check out south of Naples, and Caroline's supposed to zip over to Barcelona, but we could both reschedule and stay here in Salzburg."

Caught in a trap of his own making, Cal left it to Devon to answer. He'd wanted to make Christmas special for her but hadn't planned on sharing her right through New Year's.

To his relief, she shook her head. "I appreciate you coming over early more than you can know, but you'd better take care of business next week."

"The perfect segue," Cal commented. He started to say more but held off when he spotted Caroline coming toward them.

She reminded him very much of his sister Rebecca. Same dark hair, same intelligent eyes, same quiet air. Becky's calm, unflappable nature had served her well as the middle of the five Logan offspring. She'd fallen naturally into the role of peacemaker and negotiator between her younger and older siblings.

From the little Devon had told him about her partners, however, Cal sensed Caroline's reserve owed less to birth order and more to some traumatic event that had turned her inward and forced her to draw on a reservoir of hidden strength. Whatever the crucible was, it had molded her into a woman he suspected could more than hold her own against her partners' more outgoing personalities.

He rose to greet her and pull out a chair. When she was settled and four coffee cups had clinked together in a Christmas toast, Cal made a casual comment.

"Devon mentioned you're an opera buff. I saw something about a candlelight performance of Mozart's works at St. Peter's tonight."

"The Mozart Dinner Concert. It's world renowned." Caroline's eyes lit up. "The singers dress in traditional costume and perform excerpts from his most famous works. The food is supposedly traditional, too. Authentic dishes from Mozart's era."

Cal blinked at the transformation. When she shed her reserve and opened up, Caroline Walters was a knockout. The warm glow faded almost as quickly as it had come, however.

"I wanted to go the year Devon and Sabrina and I were at the university, but the tickets were way out of a lowly student's price range."

"That's the *only* concert she didn't drag us to," Sabrina said with a chuckle. "We had Mozart oozing out our pores that year."

"Maybe we should correct the omission," Cal suggested.

"I wish!" Caroline said fervently. "Unfortunately, the dinner concerts are sold out months in advance."

"That's what they told me when I asked about tickets."

"When did you do that?" Devon wanted to know.

"Last night, when you were having your girl time." He scratched his chin. "All they had left were seats at the prince's table. We'll have to share it with some ambassador and his entourage. I hope that's okay."

Three glances zinged his way. Caroline's expressed astonished delight. Sabrina's glinted with approval. Devon's held a glow that made Cal's chest squeeze.

Damn! He had it bad. If he hadn't already decided on a very personal, very intimate merger with Ms.

Devon McShay, he would have drawn up the articles of incorporation on the spot.

Too bad they'd been interrupted a few moments ago. He might have had the deal already signed and sealed. Later, he promised himself. First, they had another piece of unfinished business to take care of.

"We were just discussing plans for next week," he said to Caroline. "I understand you're flying to Barcelona, and Sabrina's heading to Italy to scout locations for a new contract EBS just landed. That leaves Devon to work the Logan Aerospace conference." He shifted his gaze to the woman beside him. "You *are* going to work it, aren't you?"

Devon felt the last of her defenses crumble. Like she was going to leave Cal in a lurch after all the trouble he'd gone to for her?

"I am. Sabrina and Caro and I talked about it last night."

"Good."

She still had reservations about mixing personal with professional. As she'd told Cal repeatedly, she wasn't good at compartmentalizing. But—as he'd told *her*—it didn't make sense to turn down a lucrative corporate contract just because she had a thing for the CEO.

Make that a major thing, she amended. She wasn't sure whether Cal's speech a few moments ago about spending Sunday mornings together had been a proposal or a proposition. At this point, she didn't really care.

She could admit it now. She'd fallen completely, helplessly, wholly in love with the man—as she intended to tell him when they had a few minutes alone to resume their interrupted conversation.

That might not be for a while, she realized when Cal offered a suggestion.

"Should I fly some of my people over to help with the arrangements?"

"No!"

The protest came from all three women simultaneously. Amused, he glanced from one to the other before addressing Devon.

"Are you sure? With Sabrina in Italy and Caroline in Spain, you might need assistance."

"I can handle it," she said firmly.

"Maybe the three of us could sit down with you for a few hours," Sabrina suggested. "If we hammer out some of the details, Caro and I could help Devon with the preliminary legwork before we leave tomorrow afternoon. I know it's Christmas, but…"

"No problem," Cal said easily. "Do you want to do it now?"

"Not now," Devon said with a quick glance at her watch. "I haven't given you your Christmas present yet. Sabrina and Caro helped me pick it out."

He waggled his brows. "You mean I'm getting more than what you gave me in the shower this morning?"

"Yes, you idiot." Devon ignored her friends' wide grins and pushed back her chair. "But only if we get our butts in gear. If we don't hurry, we'll miss it."

"Miss what?"

"You'll see." Like a general marshalling her troops, she barked out orders. "Everyone get their coats, hats and gloves. Be down in the lobby in ten minutes."

Cal pestered her like a kid shaking an unwrapped present, but Devon refused to give him a hint about where they were going. His got his first clue when they rounded a corner and stopped at a ticket booth.

"Wait right here," Devon ordered.

She was back a few minutes later with four tickets for the old-fashioned, cogwheel train that took visitors to the fortress perched high above Salzburg.

"Perfect timing," she announced as the train came rattling down the steep incline.

"You're sure about this?" Cal asked, eyeing the iron cars and narrow track doubtfully.

"We're sure."

When she pointed a finger at the entry gate, Caro and Sabrina hooked their arms in his and marched him forward. Their breath steamed on the frosty air as the cog train creaked and groaned its way up the steep incline. Eight nerve-wracking minutes later, they emerged onto the battlements of the fortress perched high above Salzburg.

"The fortress was constructed in 1077," Devon told Cal. "It's the largest in Europe to remain intact."

"I can see why. These rampart walls must be twenty, thirty feet thick. Who built them?"

"The archbishops who used to rule Salzburg in princely splendor. Unfortunately, the museum and the archbishop's apartments are closed today."

"Trust me," Sabrina murmured in an aside to Cal. "Closed is good. Otherwise a certain former history professor would keep you here all day."

"Philistine," Devon said, making a face at her friend.

"If the museum's closed, what's the big attraction?"

The three women exchanged smug looks and steered him around a corner.

"This."

"Good God!"

Cal's stunned reaction was exactly what Devon had hoped for. She'd wracked her brains for something to give him. Choosing a gift for a multibillionaire wasn't easy, particularly since most of the stores had shut down before she and Cal returned from their excursion to Oberndorf. Sabrina and Caro's unexpected arrival had nixed any hope of last-minute shopping, but Devon knew she *had* to give him something after all he'd given her. After consulting her friends, she hit on the perfect gift.

"This is amazing," Cal murmured as he took in the breath-stealing view.

All of Salzburg lay below, showcased against snow-covered Alps. The ramparts gave them an eagle's-eye view of the copper roofs, the narrow streets, the magnificent palaces lining the ice-coated river, the royal riding stable that hosted the world-famous music festival.

"It's our favorite place," Devon told him happily. "Caro's and Sabrina's and mine."

"Thanks for sharing it." He took her gloved hand in his and speared a glance around the small group. "All of you. It's a gift I'll always treasure."

"This is only part of it." Devon checked her watch again. "Wait five more minutes."

They spent the short wait roaming the castle walls and stamping their feet to keep out the cold. Devon's nerves ratcheted up another notch with each sweep of the second hand. Would the experience be as remarkable as she remembered? Would Cal feel the same magic she had?

Then the church bells began to toll, summoning the faithful for Christmas morning services. The great, deep-throated cathedral bells rang out first. Slowly, majestically, their booming thunder rose from the city. Then came the molten, golden knell from St. Sebastian's. Mere seconds later, silver notes poured from the bell towers of the university's four chapels. The twenty or so other churches in the city soon joined in.

This high up there weren't any buildings to block the sounds. No thick walls or double-paned windows to mute the reverberations. Every note rose liquid and clear, until the air came alive with the clang and clatter and clamor of bells.

Cal spun in a slow circle, speechless with amazement. Good thing, since Devon couldn't have heard a word above the joyous symphony. It lasted for a good five minutes before gradually tapering off.

"That," Cal said when the last echoes finally died, "was incredible."

Devon beamed, Caroline let out a contented sigh and Sabrina raised a gloved hand for a high five.

"Mission accomplished," she announced. "Now let's head back down. I'm freezing my ass off."

The rest of the day passed in a blur of whirlwind activity. The Christmas dinner prepared by the innkeeper's wife more than lived up to expectations. Stuffed to the gills, Cal and Devon set up a temporary command post in their room and spent three hours hammering out preliminaries for the Logan Aerospace/Hauptmann Iron Works conference. They broke at five to get ready for the Mozart concert and their second feast of the day. Sabrina and Caro had just left when Cal's cell phone rang.

He glanced at the number on the caller-ID screen. Devon saw his brows snap together and wondered why he didn't answer but hesitated to ask.

The phone rang again a few minutes later. This time Cal swore under his breath. When he lifted his gaze to Devon's again, his blue eyes held a combination of resignation and regret.

"It's Alexis. I'm sorry. I need to take this."

"No problem. I'll get cleaned up."

She headed into the bathroom to give him some privacy but had to conduct a fierce inner struggle before conquering the nasty urge to leave the door open a crack.

She wasn't worried about a call from his former fiancée. Cal said it was over between him and Alexis St. Germaine. Devon believed him.

There was no reason for the old doubts to surface while she freshened her makeup and dragged a brush through her hair. Even less reason for her throat to close when she emerged from the bathroom to find Cal shrugging into his overcoat.

"What's going on?"

"Alexis is here."

"In Salzburg?"

He jerked the coat to settle it over his shoulders. The movement was impatient, almost angry.

"One of my sisters told her I'd decided to spend the holidays skiing."

"So she flew over to join you on the slopes?"

"She says she has an urgent business matter to discuss." His gaze locked on hers. "One that concerns you."

"Me?"

"She's at the Emperor Charles Augustus Hotel," he said brusquely. "I remember seeing it when we were out walking yesterday."

"It's just two blocks from here," Devon confirmed, wondering what the heck this was about.

Did Alexis St. Germaine want to utilize the services of EBS? If so, why hadn't she contacted Devon directly? And what would be so urgent about that?

Or was that just an excuse to lure Cal away? If so,

she thought with a sudden catch in her breath, he'd taken the bait quickly enough.

"I'll find out what she wants and be back as soon as I can. If I'm delayed, you and Sabrina and Caro go on to the dinner concert. I'll join you there."

He dug out his wallet and extracted a credit card. Devon stiffened, but Cal was in too much of a hurry to notice.

"I've already paid for the tickets. They're waiting at will-call. You'll need this to pick them up."

He pulled her close for a fierce, hard kiss. She didn't resist, but after the door closed she folded his American Express card in a fist so tight the edges cut into her palm. A desperate mantra kept repeating inside her head.

This wasn't the Christmas curse revisited.

Cal didn't love Alexis St. Germaine.

He'd settle this "business matter," whatever it was, and join her at the concert.

He *would!*

for not ordering a more detailed background dossier when his buddy Don recommended a firm that could handle all the arrangements for Cal's short-notice trip to Germany. The brief his people had scrambled to put together on EBS had covered only the basics. Length of time in operation. Current corporate assets. Educational background and experience levels of the three owners.

Cal believed in giving small businesses a break. Hell, that's how he'd gotten his start. The personal recommendation from Don had cinched the matter.

He knew now he should have had his people dig a little deeper. Or pumped Devon for more information about herself. If he had, he might have been better prepared for whatever Alexis was going to hit him with.

Instead, he'd gone with his gut. He'd wanted Devon McShay since the moment he'd spotted her at the Dresden airport. Intent on having her, he'd brushed aside her protests that things were moving too fast, that they needed to get to know each other. Arrogant ass that he was, he'd forged ahead with his campaign to get her into his bed and keep her there.

That arrogance may well have put her at risk. Cal's prominence in the aerospace industry had provided great fodder for the media over the years. His engagement to high-profile Alexis St. Germaine had generated far more intrusive and gossipy articles.

Devon would be subject to the same intrusive scrutiny. The tabloids would dive into her past, speculate on her broken marriage, probably interview her ex, maybe even the parents she said were still so bitter and angry with each other.

Cal should have warned her, should have made sure she was ready when word of their holiday abroad leaked, as it surely would. And *he* sure as hell should have been prepared for someone to dig up a little dirt. That the someone was evidently Alexis only added to his self-disgust.

Kicking himself all over again, Cal strode up to the hotel's grand entrance. A doorman uniformed in a red jacket and black top hat swished open the brass-and-glass door.

"*Fröliche Weinachten.*"

His scowl easing, Cal returned the man's greeting.

"Merry Christmas. Could you point me to the house phones, please?"

"Yes, sir. They are just there, beside the concierge's desk."

"Thanks."

Cal barely noted the combination of soaring glass windows, crystal chandeliers and elegant nineteenth-century antiques as he strode to the bank of phones and asked to be connected to Alexis's room.

"It's Cal," he bit out when she answered.

"Come up." Her husky contralto flowed like dark velvet. "I'm in three twenty-five."

"You come down." He glanced around, spotted a casual gathering place showcased by the two-story windows. "I'll meet you in the lobby bar."

"Oh, darling." Amusement rippled through her

smoky voice. "Don't tell me you're afraid to be alone with me."

"The lobby bar, Alexis."

He snagged a table by the windows and ordered a scotch. From long experience he knew his ex-fiancée would take her time making an appearance.

Impatience ate at him while he waited. Outside the brightly lit bar, traffic had picked up. A steady stream of cars and taxis moved along the wide boulevard fronting the river. Many, Cal guessed, were headed for the concert hall.

He checked his watch, smothered a curse and downed a swallow of scotch. Thankfully, Alexis stepped out of the elevators a moment later.

Heads turned as she crossed the lobby. Tall, silvery blond and movie-star glamorous in a peacock blue cape trimmed in fur dyed to match, she swept into the bar.

"Merry Christmas, darling."

"You, too, Alexis."

Her scent enveloped him as she stretched up for a kiss. Cal brushed her cheek instead of her lush red lips. Her eyes mocked him as she took the chair he held out for her.

"I wish you'd told me you were planning on a skiing break," she said, arranging the cape in graceful folds. "You know I love to ski. Remember the week we spent in St. Moritz?"

"I remember."

Cal signaled to the waitress and took his seat.

Once she'd taken Alexis's order for a champagne cocktail, he cut straight to the chase.

"What's this about?"

"So direct," she murmured, her red lips forming a little moue. "So abrupt. You don't have time for more than a hello and goodbye after I flew all this way to see you?"

"Actually, I don't." He relaxed into a wry grin. "I'm doing Mozart tonight."

"Darling!" The moue became a teasing pout. "And here I had to promise you all kinds of carnal delights to convince you to escort me to a concert."

Not quite, but Cal let that pass.

"Your little travel planner must be quite something to get you to a Mozart concert."

"She is, and her name is Devon. Devon McShay, as you know perfectly well."

"Yes, I do."

The waitress arrived then with the champagne. Alexis held up the crystal flute, clinked it against his glass and took a sip. Over the rim of the glass her glance was amused and just a little malicious.

"The question is, how much do you know about her?"

"All I need to."

"Are you sure?"

"Before this conversation goes any further, Alexis, I want to make one thing clear."

He kept his smile easy and his tone even but made damned sure she got the message.

"I'm not paying you for whatever dirt you've dug up on Devon. And I strongly suggest you don't sell it to the tabloids."

"Oh, Cal. You wound me. Do you think I would do that?"

Her limpid, wide-eyed innocence was so exaggerated he had to laugh.

"I know damned well you would. For the right price. Just remember, it's not too late to stop the transfer of the Park Avenue apartment into your name."

A blood-red nail tapped against the champagne flute. Once. Twice. Three times. Then she gave a low, throaty laugh that drew the interested glance of every male in the bar.

"Ah, well. It was worth a try."

Her amusement fading, she took another sip of champagne. Cal waited, guessing that she couldn't resist dropping whatever bombshell she'd come to deliver. He knew he'd guessed right when she slanted him a sly glance.

"Did Ms. McShay happen to mention her father is an accountant?"

"As a matter of fact, she did."

"Did she also happen to mention that he's with Pendleton and Smith?"

Cal's eyes narrowed. "No," he said slowly, "she didn't."

Her mouth curved in a smile of malicious satisfaction. "I thought not."

P&S was one of the largest accounting firms on the

East Coast. Among their most prominent clients was Templeton Systems, Logan Aerospace's chief competitor in the drive to acquire Hauptmann Metal Works.

"Is that what you flew all this way to tell me, Alexis? That Devon's father works for my competitor? If so, you're too late. I've closed the deal I was working."

Disappointment etched hard lines into her face, making it look years older for a moment. Her nail tapped the champagne glass again.

"Well, I was going to share a few details of her rather messy divorce, but I think I'll let you ferret those out for yourself."

"Wise decision."

She inclined her head, acknowledging defeat with a careless grace that took the edge from his anger. Softening his expression, Cal pushed back his chair.

"I'm sorry to leave you alone on Christmas night, but…"

"I know, I know. You're doing Mozart."

Her sultry charm returned as she rose with him. "Go," she ordered with another of her throaty chuckles. "I won't be alone for long."

Her glance swept past him to engage that of the silver-maned gentleman at the next table. The seductive smile she sent the man almost made him choke on his bourbon.

"No," Cal agreed with a grin. "You won't. Goodbye, Alexis."

"Goodbye, my darling."

She made sure he didn't take this kiss on the

cheek. Framing his face with both hands, she surrounded him with her unique aura of sex and sin.

He caught her wrists. Intent on extracting himself, Cal didn't notice the traffic backed up on the street outside the brightly illuminated bar, much less Caroline's white, shocked face framed in the rear window of a taxi.

Thirteen

Devon barely registered Caroline's dismayed gasp, quickly smothered. Nor did she pay any attention to Sabrina's soft "Damn!"

She sat frozen, her entire being focused on the two people on the other side of the soaring glass windows. The image imprinted itself on every brain cell. She could see it with excruciating clarity even after the stalled taxi began to move and her two friends swung toward her.

"Dev?"

She shook her head, too numb to speak. Sabrina swore again, viciously. Caro groped for her hand and squeezed so hard the bones ground together.

"Oh, Dev. It's not what it looked like. It can't be."

Still she couldn't speak. Caro leaned across her to throw an agonized glance at Sabrina.

"Tell her! Cal isn't Blake. He's not anything like Blake."

"Bull." Sabrina was too angry to pull her punches. "All men have one thing on their minds. You know it. I know it. Devon, unfortunately, has now experienced a double dose of reality."

"There's… There's probably a perfectly good explanation for what we just saw," Caro said stubbornly.

"Yeah, sure."

"Dammit, Sabrina! You're not helping here."

"I don't want to help. I want to pound Cal Logan's face into steak tartare."

"Oh, for…!"

Caro swung back, her face reflecting some of the anguish piercing Devon's chest.

"He's not Blake, Dev. You said it yourself. He's funny and smart and kind and—"

"I know." Devon tried to swallow past the brick in her throat. "I know. Just… Just give me a minute."

The minute stretched into two, then three. The numbness went away. The ache in Devon's chest didn't. It was still there, sharp and stabbing, when the taxi swept past the bridge spanning the Salzach and joined the stream of traffic turning into the yard of the concert hall.

The line of vehicles inched to the colonnaded entrance. An attendant in a white wig and blue satin knee breeches stepped forward to open the door.

Sabrina took care of the fare and joined her friends at the entrance.

"Cal's already paid for the tickets," Devon said, forcing each careful word. "They're at the will-call window."

They claimed the tickets and mingled with the crowd in the richly decorated foyer. The minutes stretched out again, slow and agonizing. Sabrina snagged glasses of champagne from a bewigged waiter and downed hers in a few angry swallows. Caro kept up a soft commentary about the pieces played by the costumed string quartet that entertained the pre-dinner crowd.

Devon's fingers tightened on the stem of her champagne goblet when a gong resonated at the top of the wide marble staircase. A footman in shining satin and white lace stepped forward with a sonorous announcement.

"Dinner is served."

She dug two tickets out of the envelope they'd picked up at the window. "You and Caro go on in. I'll wait for Cal here."

"No way!" Sabrina countered. "We'll wait with you."

"*Please.*" She thrust the tickets into her friend's reluctant hand. "Go in."

When Sabrina looked like she might balk, Caro grabbed her arm and yanked her toward the stairs.

The crowd mounted the wide marble steps and were greeted by a costumed soprano singing one of

Mozart's most famous arias. The lilting strains followed Devon as she moved to the windows at the far end of the now-empty foyer.

Outside the window, the illuminated towers and church steeples formed a timeless nightscape. Above them, spotlights lit up the majestic fortress that had guarded the city for ten centuries.

Salzburg. The city of her youthful hopes and dreams. The magical place she'd ached to share with Cal.

She hugged her arms to her chest, her gaze on the castle ramparts. And just like that her world righted itself.

The doubts faded. The hurt went away. She didn't need Caro to remind her Cal wasn't anything like Blake. She knew it. The shock of seeing him locked in an embrace with his one-time fiancée had shaken her to her core. Worse, it raised the ghosts of Christmases past.

But all Devon had to do was recall the wonder of last night at the Oberndorn chapel. Think about the calls Cal made to her friends. Remember the awe on his face when the bells sang out this morning.

He was more generous than anyone she knew and had given her more joy than she'd ever thought to experience. She knew with every fiber of her being that she couldn't be wrong about him or the feelings he roused in her.

"Devon!"

She spun around, saw him thrust his overcoat at

an attendant. Impatience and regret was stamped across his face as he hurried toward her.

"I'm sorry I'm late. Damned traffic got snarled at the bridge. Why didn't you go on in?"

"I was waiting for you."

"Are we too late for dinner?"

"Not yet." Grinning like a fool, she hooked her arm through his. "We'd better hurry, though, or we'll miss the potato soup."

"Hold on. Don't you want to hear why Alexis flew over to Salzburg?"

"Not tonight."

"Are you sure? It concerns you and—"

She stopped him by the simple expedient of laying a hand over his mouth.

"Not tonight, Cal. It's Christmas. I have food, music and friends waiting inside. And you're here, with me. That's all I want or need or care about. Everything else can wait until tomorrow."

"Not everything."

Tugging her hand aside, he smiled down at her. "About those Sunday mornings reading the paper…?"

Her heart bumped. "Yes?"

"That was my clumsy way of saying I love you."

"Glad you clarified that." Happiness spread through her, warming her from the inside out. "'Cause I love you, too."

He swept an arm around her waist and tugged her against him. Devon went into the kiss eagerly, joyfully, while Mozart's glorious aria floated from the hall above. She was breathless when he lifted his head and grinned down at her.

"You do know we're coming back to Salzburg on our honeymoon, don't you?"

"I'll work all the arrangements," she promised, laughing.

* * * * *

*Turn the page for a sneak preview
of the next installment in Merline Lovelace's
HOLIDAYS ABROAD—Sabrina's story,
THE DUKE'S NEW YEAR'S RESOLUTION,
coming from Silhouette Desire in December.
When the former party girl is run off
the road, the errant driver is fortunately
a doctor—not to mention a duke!
But Sabrina bears a strong resemblance
to the duke's "late" wife—whose body
has never been found.
Can Marco convince the seductive American
that his growing hunger for her doesn't
spring from a desire for a substitute wife?*

"Signorina! Signorina! Mi sente?"

A deep, compelling voice pierced the gray haze. Sabrina fought the agony shooting through her and put all the energy she could summon into lifting her lids.

"Ecco, brava. Apra gl'occhi."

Slowly, so slowly, a face swam into view.

"Wh-what happened?"

"Siete…" He gave a quick shake of his head and shifted to flawless English. "You fell from the road above. Luckily, this cypress broke your descent."

Sabrina blinked a twisted tree trunk into focus. Its thin branches and silvery green leaves formed a backdrop for the face hovering over her. Even dazed and confused, she felt its sensual impact.

The man was certifiably gorgeous! Whiskers darkened his cheeks and strong, square chin. His mouth could tempt a saint to sin, and Sabrina was certainly no candidate for canonization. His short black hair had just a hint of curl in it, and his skin was tanned to warm oak.

But it was his eyes that mesmerized her. Dark and compelling, they stared into hers. For an absurd moment, she had the ridiculous notion he was looking into her soul.

Then more of her haze cleared and she recognized the driver of the Ferrari. Anger spiked through her, overriding the pain.

"You almost hit me!"

She planted a hand against the tree trunk and tried to sit up. The attempt produced two immediate reactions. The first was a searing jolt that lanced from her ankle to her hip. The second was a big hand splayed against her shoulder, accompanied by a sharp order.

"Be still! You're not bleeding from any external wounds, but you may have sustained a concussion or internal injuries. Tell me, do you hurt when you breathe?"

She drew in a cautious breath. "No."

"Can you move your head?"

She tried a tentative tilt. "Yes."

"Lie still while I check for broken bones."

"Hey! Watch where you put those hands, pal."

Impatience stamped across his classic features. "I am a doctor."

Good excuse to cop a feel, Sabrina thought, too pissed to appreciate his gentle touch.

"You have no business taking these hairpin turns so fast," she informed him. "Especially when there's no guardrail. I had nowhere to go but down. If I hadn't hit this tree, I could have—ow!"

She clenched her teeth against the agony when he ran his hands down her calf to her ankle.

Frowning, the doc sat back on his heels. "With your boot on, I can't tell if the ankle is broken or merely sprained. We must get you to the hospital for X rays."

He glanced from her to the road above and back again.

"My cell phone is in the car. I can call an ambulance. Unfortunately, the closest will have to come from the town of Amalfi, thirty kilometers from here."

Terrific! Thirty kilometers of narrow, winding roads with blind curves and snaking switchbacks. She'd be down here all day, clinging to this damn tree.

"It's better if we get you to the car and I drive you to the hospital myself."

Sabrina eyed the slope doubtfully. "I don't think I'm up for a climb."

"I'll carry you."

He said it with such self-assurance that she almost believed he could. He had the shoulders for it. They looked wide and solid under his suede bomber jacket.

Sabrina was no lightweight, however. She kept in shape with daily workouts, but her five-eight height and lush curves added up to more pounds than she cared to admit in polite company.

"Thanks anyway, but I'll wait for the ambulance."

"You could black out again or go into shock." Pushing to his feet, he braced himself at an angle on the slope and issued a brusque order. "Take my hand."

The imperious command rubbed her exactly the wrong way. She'd spent a turbulent childhood and her even more tempestuous college years rebelling against her cold, autocratic father. She'd paid the price for her revolt many times over, but she still didn't take orders well.

"Anyone ever tell you that you need to work on your bedside manner, Doc? It pretty well sucks."

His dark brows snapped together in a way that said clearly he wasn't used to being taken to task by his patients. She answered with a bland smile. After a short staring contest, his scowl relaxed into a reluctant grin.

"I believe that has been mentioned to me before."

The air left Sabrina's lungs a second time. The man was seriously hot without that crooked grin.

With it, he made breathing a lost cause.

* * * * *

Here is a sneak preview of
A STONE CREEK CHRISTMAS,
the latest in Linda Lael Miller's acclaimed
McKETTRICK *series.*

A lonely horse brought vet Olivia O'Ballivan to Tanner Quinn's farm, but it's the rancher's love that might cause her to stay.

A STONE CREEK CHRISTMAS
Available December 2008
from Silhouette Special Edition.

Tanner heard the rig roll in around sunset. Smiling, he wandered to the window. Watched as Olivia O'Ballivan climbed out of her Suburban, flung one defiant glance toward the house and started for the barn, the golden retriever trotting along behind her.

Taking his coat and hat down from the peg next to the back door, he put them on and went outside. He was used to being alone, even liked it, but keeping company with Doc O'Ballivan, bristly though she sometimes was, would provide a welcome diversion.

He gave her time to reach the horse Butterpie's stall, then walked into the barn.

The golden retriever came to greet him, all

wagging tail and melting brown eyes, and he bent to stroke her soft, sturdy back. "Hey, there, dog," he said.

Sure enough, Olivia was in the stall, brushing Butterpie down and talking to her in a soft, soothing voice that touched something private inside Tanner and made him want to turn on one heel and beat it back to the house.

He'd be damned if he'd do it, though.

This was *his* ranch, *his* barn. Well-intentioned as she was, *Olivia* was the trespasser here, not him.

"She's still very upset," Olivia told him, without turning to look at him or slowing down with the brush.

Shiloh, always an easy horse to get along with, stood contentedly in his own stall, munching away on the feed Tanner had given him earlier. Butterpie, he noted, hadn't touched her supper as far as he could tell.

"Do you know anything at all about horses, Mr. Quinn?" Olivia asked.

He leaned against the stall door, the way he had the day before, and grinned. He'd practically been raised on horseback; he and Tessa had grown up on their grandmother's farm in the Texas hill country, after their folks divorced and went their separate ways, both of them too busy to bother with a couple of kids. "A few things," he said. "And I mean to call you Olivia, so you might as well return the favor and address me by my first name."

He watched as she took that in, dealt with it, decided on an approach. He'd have to wait and see what that turned out to be, but he didn't mind. It was a pleasure just watching Olivia O'Ballivan grooming a horse.

"All right, *Tanner,*" she said. "This barn is a disgrace. When are you going to have the roof fixed? If it snows again, the hay will get wet and probably mold…"

He chuckled, shifted a little. He'd have a crew out there the following Monday morning to replace the roof and shore up the walls—he'd made the arrangements over a week before—but he felt no particular compunction to explain that. He was enjoying her ire too much; it made her color rise and her hair fly when she turned her head, and the faster breathing made her perfect breasts go up and down in an enticing rhythm. "What makes you so sure I'm a greenhorn?" he asked mildly, still leaning on the gate.

At last she looked straight at him, but she didn't move from Butterpie's side. "Your hat, your boots— that fancy red truck you drive. I'll bet it's customized."

Tanner grinned. Adjusted his hat. "Are you telling me real cowboys don't drive red trucks?"

"There are lots of trucks around here," she said. "Some of them are red, and some of them are new. And *all* of them are splattered with mud or manure or both."

"Maybe I ought to put in a car wash, then," he teased. "Sounds like there's a market for one. Might be a good investment."

She softened, though not significantly, and spared him a cautious half smile, full of questions she probably wouldn't ask. "There's a good car wash in Indian Rock," she informed him. "People go there. It's only forty miles."

"Oh," he said with just a hint of mockery. "*Only* forty miles. Well, then. Guess I'd better dirty up my truck if I want to be taken seriously in these here parts. Scuff up my boots a bit, too, and maybe stomp on my hat a couple of times."

Her cheeks went a fetching shade of pink. "You are twisting what I said," she told him, brushing Butterpie again, her touch gentle but sure. "I meant…"

Tanner envied that little horse. Wished he had a furry hide, so he'd need brushing, too.

"You *meant* that I'm not a real cowboy," he said. "And you could be right. I've spent a lot of time on construction sites over the last few years, or in meetings where a hat and boots wouldn't be appropriate. Instead of digging out my old gear, once I decided to take this job, I just bought new."

"I bet you don't even *have* any old gear," she challenged, but she was smiling, albeit cautiously, as though she might withdraw into a disapproving frown at any second.

He took off his hat, extended it to her. "Here," he teased. "Rub that around in the muck until it suits you."

She laughed, and the sound—well, it caused a powerful and wholly unexpected shift inside him. Scared the hell out of him and, paradoxically, made him yearn to hear it again.

* * * * *

Discover how this rugged rancher's wanderlust
is tamed in time for a merry Christmas, in
A STONE CREEK CHRISTMAS.
In stores December 2008.

Silhouette®

SPECIAL EDITION™

FROM *NEW YORK TIMES* BESTSELLING AUTHOR

LINDA LAEL MILLER

A STONE CREEK CHRISTMAS

Veterinarian Olivia O'Ballivan finds the animals in Stone Creek playing Cupid between her and Tanner Quinn. Even Tanner's daughter, Sophie, is eager to play matchmaker. With everyone conspiring against them and the holiday season fast approaching, Tanner and Olivia may just get everything they want for Christmas after all!

*Available December 2008
wherever books are sold.*

REQUEST YOUR FREE BOOKS!

2 FREE NOVELS PLUS 2 FREE GIFTS!

Passionate, Powerful, Provocative!

COMING NEXT MONTH

**#1909 THE BILLIONAIRE IN PENTHOUSE B—
Anna DePalo**
Park Avenue Scandals
Who's the mystery man in Penthouse B? She's determined to uncover his every secret. *He's* determined to get her under his covers!

#1910 THE TYCOON'S SECRET—Kasey Michaels
Gifts from a Billionaire
He's kept his identity under wraps and hired her to decorate his billion-dollar mansion. But when seduction turns serious, will the truth tear them apart?

#1911 QUADE'S BABIES—Brenda Jackson
The Westmorelands
This sexy Westmoreland gets more than he bargained for when he discovers he's a daddy—times three! Now he's determined to do the right thing…if she'll have him.…

#1912 THE THROW-AWAY BRIDE—Ann Major
Golden Spurs
A surprise pregnancy and a marriage of convenience brought them together. Can their newfound love survive the secrets he's been keeping from her?

**#1913 THE DUKE'S NEW YEAR'S RESOLUTION—
Merline Lovelace**
Holidays Abroad
Initially stunned by her resemblance to his late wife, the Italian duke is reluctant to invite her to his villa, but it doesn't take long for him to invite her into his bed.

#1914 PREGNANCY PROPOSAL—Tessa Radley
The Saxon Brides
She's the girl he's always secretly loved—and is his late brother's fiancée. When he learns she's pregnant, he proposes—having no idea she's really carrying *his* baby!